Whackadoodle Times

Also by Kim Antieau

Novels

The Blue Tail • *Broken Moon* • *Butch* • *Church of the Old Mermaids*
Coyote Cowgirl • *Deathmark* • *The Desert Siren* • *The Fish Wife*
Her Frozen Wild • *The Gaia Websters* • *Jewelweed Station*
The Jigsaw Woman • *Maternal Instincts* • *Mercy, Unbound*
The Monster's Daughter • *Queendom: Feast of the Saints*
The Rift • *Ruby's Imagine* • *Swans in Winter*
Whackadoodle Times Two

Nonfiction

Answering the Creative Call
*Certified: Learning to Repair Myself and the World
in the Emerald City*
Counting on Wildflowers: An Entanglement
Old Mermaids Book of Days and Nights
The Salmon Mysteries: a Reimagining of the Eleusinian Mysteries
*The Salmon Mysteries Workbook: Reimagining the
Eleusinian Mysteries*
Under the Tucson Moon

Collections

Entangled Realities (with Mario Milosevic)
The First Book of Old Mermaids Tales
Haunted
Tales Fabulous and Fairy
Trudging to Eden

Chapbook

Blossoms

Blog

www.kimantieau.com

Photography

kimantieau.smugmug.com

WHACKADOODLE TIMES

KIM ANTIEAU

Green Snake
PUBLISHING

Whackadoodle Times
by Kim Antieau

Copyright © 2012 by Kim Antieau

ISBN-13: 978-1-949644-05-0

Cover image copyright © Eduard Stelmakh | Dreamstime.com
Book design by Mario Milosevic and Kim Antieau.
Special thanks to Nancy Milosevic, Tracie Jones, and Ruth Ford Biersdorf.

Published by Green Snake Publishing
www.greensnakepublishing.com

for

Guy Boss,

who laughed

ONE

I know exactly when things changed. Most people can't point to the time and place when life went whackadoodle. I can. I suppose if I were introspective I might be able to look back in time and say that life as we knew it started to dissolve when Henry Ford made the car. Or when God made man. Or Goddess made woman. Or when the first two haploid gametes fused to become a zygote.

Or when I got married. Had children. Became filled with ennui. Lived the dissipated life.

Only I wasn't filled with ennui—grief, maybe, but not ennui—and my life wasn't any more or less dissipated than anyone else's. At least anyone else on my block.

Which could have been part of the problem. I didn't exactly live on a block. More like an enclave. Or a bunch of big houses in an area that could be called a canyon, mountain, or hill. All of it slip-sliding into the ocean that was getting closer every day. But I digress. I babble. Thus my father's nickname for me:

Brook. I added the "e" for fun when I was in college. I thought that would stop my classmates from asking me if my brother's name was "Up a Creek" or "Down the River."

It wasn't a very good college.

Anyway, it began once upon a time, I suppose, the day Hayword and I were sitting out by the pool. It was a beautiful bluish kind of day. (We were close to la-la land at the time, so how blue could it be? It's what the locals call fog and the scientists call the Earth going to Hell in a hand basket—or in a designer handbag, given we were in Californ-eye-eh.)

Hayword was working on a script. Yes, I was married to a Hollywood writer—had been one myself for a while. And he was such a cliché, really. One day he was in great demand; the next day no one would return his calls. This made him slightly neurotic and a bit moody. Some might say he was manic-depressive, but he was not. (Can't a person drink to blackout some days and cry uncontrollably other days without being labeled?)

Not that Hayword ever drank to a blackout or cried uncontrollably.

Someone in our house did that, but I don't think it was Hayword.

On this particular day, Hayword was working on the rewrite of *Powerbreakers,* a script that had already sold. He had gotten the money, so he was on his way to the stage when he started to feel guilty over the massive amount of filthy lucre he received for writing down lies. That was how he characterized it. When he was talking to a stud head, he waxed on about story and drama and point of view. When he groused to me, Hayword said he was merely taking out a book from his library of lies—i.e., his brain—and transcribing it.

Hayword had more guilt about the good life than anyone I had ever met.

He was like that when we were kids, too. I'd known him

since we were in elementary school. He was a little kid—until he hit about thirteen. Then he sprouted up like a big old sunflower. (I'm spinning some corn now because I did grow up in the Midwest.)

Even when he was little he was always standing up for some cause or some kid, going toe to toe with the bullies that were twice his size. And then there was me, his best friend, motioning the head bully over to me to convince him it would be much more lucrative to let Hayword go. In return, I gave them the answers to some test or paid them a couple of bucks for a week. I'd try to convince Hayword to shut up, but he never would. At least back then. Felt it was his obligation.

Meanwhile, I was paying off his debts.

I was glad when he got tall.

We were sitting by the pool together and the doorbell rang. We both got up to answer it. Hayword may have wanted a break from the manuscript—or maybe he was trying to get away from me. I had been talking about our daughter Fern who was working on her master's degree in psychology up in Santa Barbara. (I named her Fern because I wanted to carry on the woodland fiction that began with my name. Was Fern grounded, rooted or feathery and wild like her name? No. She was mean. Hadn't liked me since I birthed her, as far as I could tell.)

Hayword and I, along with our twelve-year-old son David, lived in an exclusive neighborhood where we knew all our neighbors, and unfortunately, they knew us. We attended each other's birthday parties, our children's weddings, and any backyard barbecues, and we occasionally slept with each other's spouses. And by "we," I mean "they." Personally, I'd seen too many of them naked and heard their views on too many subjects to be interested in having sex with any of them.

What I'm saying is that we knew the people in our 'hood. Still, Hayword should not have opened our front door without even looking through the peephole. We did have a gate; Hayword must have left it open. He wanted to pretend he was still that boy from the Midwest who knew and liked everyone. A boy from the Midwest who believed in the goodness of everyone. Every time he started dancing down this particular nostalgic yellow-brick road, I reminded him that he grew up fifty miles from Detroit, which was the murder capital of the world when we were kids.

"Not murder capital of the world," he'd say. "Just murder capital of the United States."

Hayword opened the front door. A startling-looking woman stood on our threshold. She wasn't dressed like a bag lady, but she was not dressed like anyone I had ever seen in la-la land or environs. She was Caucasian. (I hate that word. Sounds like something out of a police bulletin. That was how I looked at her just then. I wanted to memorize her features in case I had to describe her to a police sketch artist.) So she was white. Probably Irish. English. One of those pale tribes. Yet her skin was slightly brown, as though she'd been climbing a mountain or windsurfing. You know what I mean. She had that burnished look of someone who was outdoors a great deal. Her brown hair was pulled away from her head into those nasty Rasta braids. And she wore some kind of dress—truly nondescript—with pants on beneath it. She had a huge bag slung over her shoulder.

She did look like a bag lady. Or what I imagined a bag lady looked like. It had been a long while since I had been anywhere bag ladies roamed.

This woman looked at us with clear blue eyes and said, "You got a pool house?"

Conventional wisdom holds that women are sentimental suckers. Let me tell ya: It ain't so. It's men. They are such soft touches. Especially when it comes to women. Hayword was no exception. I don't mean he was leering at this woman. She was probably only a few years younger than I was. Men don't lust after women my age much, at least not in this town. She looked smart, like she had all her marbles. Hayword probably assumed she was down on her luck. I figured she was selling something.

Whatever it was, I wasn't buying.

Hayword was.

"Sure, we got a pool house," he said. "Why?"

I groaned. Whenever he was fully onto the path of the guilty rich guy, he wanted to do good deeds to assuage his conscience.

"It's not a pool house," I said. Hayword looked at me. "It's more of a garden house."

"Garden?" Hayword asked.

"I'm going to put in a garden," I said. Some freaking day I was going to put in a freaking garden.

"So you have a garden house?" the woman asked.

The wind shifted then, and let's just say that this woman standing on our threshold was a little earthy-smelling. Musky. Sweaty. Not sweat that has turned. But that rich sweaty smell you like on your lover but not on a stranger.

"Look, Eartha," I said, "whatever you're selling—"

"I'm not selling," she said. "And how did you know my name? My father nicknamed me Earth because I smelled like dirt. I added the 'a' so it wouldn't be so strange. But then people nicknamed me Eartha Kitten. I didn't really like that. Eartha Cat I can dig. Eartha Jaguar. Eartha Cougar." She was looking at me, but I could tell she was paying attention to my husband, too. "I would like to stay in your garden house for a while," she said. "I'm a traveller, and I need a rest."

"Just like that?" I asked.

"In exchange," she said, "I will do one great thing a day for you."

I looked at my husband. He was smiling. A sly smile. He loved these kinds of distractions.

"Oh yeah?" he said. "What one great thing would you do today?"

"Let me see the garden house, and then I'll decide."

"Okay," Hayword said.

"Hayword," I said. "Are you crazy?"

"Excuse us," he said. "My wife and I need to discuss this."

He shut the door gently, with Eartha on one side and us on the other. I stood looking at him with my hands on my hips, like some stereotypical woman in some bad movie who was always ruining the fun of her infantile husband.

"Brooke," he said. "This is gold, gold! We're locked up in this huge house where we never experience real life. Here's someone offering to do one great thing for us. Even if it's only for today, don't you want to see what it is? Just for fun?" He grinned. "Come on. In the old days, you'd walk a mile for a good time."

"And I'd walk ten miles away from a bad one," I said.

"Let's see where it goes," he said. "Might make a good movie."

"She could be a psychopath," I said. "A serial killer."

"I'll make sure she's not," he said.

He opened the door again. Eartha Kitten was still standing there.

"We'll let you do one great thing," he said, "and then we'll see. First, though, we need to know that you're not a psychopath, a serial killer, or on the FBI's most wanted list."

"Oh, good lord," I said. "Just stamp sucker on our foreheads."

Eartha held her bag out to Hayword. "You can check for weapons," she said.

Hayword didn't take the bag. Neither did I. If this were a movie, millions of people in the audience would be screaming, "Don't, don't, don't let her in, you idiot!"

Well, maybe not *millions* of people.

She slung the bag over her shoulder again.

"My name is Eartha Jefferson."

I squinted. Her real name could not be Eartha. She was playing me.

She seemed to be waiting to hear who we were. I didn't say a word. Hayword moved out of the way so she could come inside.

"First, the one great thing," he said.

Eartha stepped into our house. I shook my head. Hayword was going to learn to lock that goddamn gate if I had to shoot him to get him to remember.

My daft husband led the way through the house and out the back to the pool. Eartha didn't look to her left or to her right. She wasn't obviously casing the joint. We walked along the pool and a bit away from the house to the garden house. Hayword opened the door and let Eartha go in first.

I stayed outside.

"Go sit by the pool," this strange woman said. "I'll be right out with the one great thing." She handed Hayword her bag. He took it this time. He looked at me and grinned. If I hadn't been so annoyed with him, I would have laughed.

We went back to the pool and sat in the lounge chairs. Hayword started looking at manuscript pages again. I lay back and wondered if I could really put a garden somewhere back near the pool house. I kept looking over my shoulder to see what Eartha was doing. Probably sticking our valuables under her baggy dress.

And then she came out of the pool house—garden house—carrying two filled martini glasses. She handed one to me and the other to Hayword. I looked at the drink. It was slightly darker than any martini I had ever had. And the glass was warm. Room-temperature.

"This is your one great thing?" I asked.

"How do you know we're not both recovering alcoholics?" Hayword asked, "and if I drank this it would end a decade-long dry spell?"

"If that's the case," she said, "you might want to do something about that garden house. If you named a place by what was inside it, you'd have to call it the liquor cabinet, not a garden house."

Hayword laughed.

"There is one caveat," Eartha said. "You have a choice. This will be the one great thing for the day. And there are only two glasses of this drink. One each. Once you drink it, it's done. It's over. I cannot make another. This one great thing will be gone forever. Do you understand?"

I frowned. I wasn't sure I understood.

Hayword said, "Sure."

He downed his martini. Just like that. I yelled his name to stop him, but it was too late. She could have poisoned it. She could have put drugs in it. She could have done anything to it. We had no idea.

"Oh, man," Hayword said. "What did you do, Eartha? Brooke, you've got to taste this."

I sighed.

"She's waiting to see if you'll go down," Eartha said.

"What?" Hayword asked. "Oh." He laughed and looked at me. "I don't think she poisoned it."

I smelled my drink. The scent of juniper went up my nostrils and seemed to tickle my brain a bit. I closed my eyes, carefully brought the glass up to my lips, and took a sip.

For a moment, I thought I was in a forest. I could smell the pine trees. I could feel the slight chill of the snow on the floor of the forest. And somewhere, someone was brewing hot chocolate.

The martini had a slight sweet taste of chocolate.

"Just the right amount of gin and vermouth," Hayword said. "And maybe lemon? I love lemon. Or orange. I wish I had savored it. That is a continual lesson for me to learn. Savor, savor, savor."

I took another sip.

It was the best drink I had ever tasted.

I held my glass out to Hayword.

"No," Eartha said. "One each. That's yours."

"Do you want the rest of it?" I asked.

"I don't drink," she said. "So do we have a deal?"

Hayword looked at me. I looked back at him.

"I want to see some ID," he said to Eartha. "And then we'll take it one day at a time. One great thing at a time."

"Good," she said.

Hayword stood and reached out his hand to her. "I'm Hayword," he said, "and this is Brooke."

"Nice to meet you," she said. "And now, I've been walking for a long while. I'd like to rest."

"I'll show you where everything is," Hayword said.

He picked up her bag, and together they went into the garden house.

I sat in my lounge chair looking at the martini. It was absolutely the best thing I had ever drank. I suddenly felt like that little boy in *The Lion, the Witch, and the Wardrobe* who wants more of the magical Turkish delight the White Witch feeds him. I wanted to keep drinking this liquid forever. I felt so relaxed after two sips. Happy. Contented. I wanted more. And more.

I stared at the gulp of drink left in the bottom of the glass.

Who did she think she was creating something like this and only making enough for two drinks?

I was no Edmund Peevish in Narnia. Or whatever his name was. And she wasn't the White Witch.

I tossed the rest of the drink in the straggly bush next to me.
I gasped. What had I done?
And then I licked my lips.

TWO

I didn't sleep very well that night. I kept getting up and looking out our window to see what I could see in the garden house. Didn't see anything. Which made me very suspicious. Maybe Eartha was sitting inside the house, in the dark, figuring out where to plant the listening devices so she could spy on us.

I even went into David's room and looked through his window. He sleeps through almost everything, including me tripping over whatever crap he has on his floor.

I still didn't see anything.

Except for David's electronic whatever flashing under his sheets. I took it out, turned it off, and put it on his desk. Shouldn't have those things so close to his body so much of the time. He was going to grow an extra appendage.

Or become as obnoxious as his sister.

I couldn't see Eartha or any of her kittens from David's window either.

I had tried to recreate her martini—even though I didn't ordinarily like martinis—so it was possible my psycho-detector was registering more than usual. I was a paranoid drunk.

I slept through breakfast and David and Hayword heading out for the day. Hayword took David to his private school. We'd sent Fern to public school—because we were idiots trying to remain "grounded in our Midwest values" or some such shit. But Fern could take care of herself. Someone picked on her, she'd punch them. Or outwit them with her words. She could be very cruel. In fact, for all we knew, she was one of the bullies going after poor defenseless kids like David.

David was nearly ten years younger than Fern, and we knew when he was an infant that he would have to go to school someplace special. Nurturing. He was a good kid with a soft heart. Sometimes I thought it was because his little brother Alberto died when David was two. He cried for about a year after his brother died.

We hardly ever talk about Alberto.

Or what happened afterward. I was a bit depressed and Hayword decided to fuck some woman in his office. She was a young blond actress who wanted him to write a movie for her. I imagine. I don't really know. He fucked her. I saw it all. Said I'd kill him if he ever did it again. He begged my forgiveness, swore it was his grief, and blah, blah, blah. I let him come home.

David still cried for a year.

After that, I told Hayword I needed a space of my own. You know, like Virginia Woolf. I even quoted Virginia Woolf when I was talking to him. Said if I didn't get a fucking room of my own, I was going to walk into the sea with bricks in my pockets.

Not that I was asking for Hayword's permission. We had come to California together as a collaborating couple. Got some points on our very first little film, *Love and Other Insanities,* so we made a mint right off the bat.

Hayword really got into the Hollywood thing. He liked to schmooze and bullshit with all the other Hollywood people. Gawd. I hated it. They'd smile to your face and promise you the moon and the next day they'd sell you out or stab you in the back or whatever metaphor you want to use to indicate that on the whole they were a bunch of lying, thieving assholes. At least the ones with money.

Of course that is a gross generality. It's a gross generality based on my experiences. I'm not social in that way. And I didn't like trying to figure out everyone's motives all the time. So I stopped doing the circuit—as it were—and stopped going to meetings, concentrated on raising the one kid who couldn't stand me and on birthing a couple of others, one who died and another who was a bit more fragile than was good for—well, good for me. Hayword was already a handful. He wanted constant reassurance from me. Christ, I can't tell you how many times I wanted to tell him to grow a pair. I knew if his self-esteem went down, I'd be the one propping it back up, and I was tired of it.

Anyway, David went to a school he liked where the teachers nurtured him and the other students seemed to like him. Hayword took him to school some days; I took him other days. When I couldn't or didn't feel like it or I was late getting to my art studio, I sometimes asked Violeta to take him. Violeta was our housekeeper slash cook.

After I told Hayword I needed a room of my own, I found a house close to the village. It was a small old style ranch house from the 1930s. White with dark green shutters. White picket fence. Looked so California out under tall old sycamore trees, like a place Carol Lombard and Clark Gable would have lived. So I got it. I bought an easel and some paints, pencils, chalk. All the best material. My intentions were pure.

Thing was, I wasn't any kind of artist and never have been. I was a pretty good writer when Hayword and I started out. A commercial writer. I knew what kind of scripts to write to create a play or a movie that people would like. Not great art but something entertaining with a bit of heart.

But I was not an artist, not someone who used a brush and paints. It didn't matter: Hayword was so guilt-ridden about his affair he never questioned my artistic endeavors.

My Enclave neighbors, at least the female ones, called my art studio my love nest. I never confirmed or denied. Although sometimes I let on that I didn't love anyone who came there, but I was fond of all of them.

And today, one of the ones I was quite fond of was stopping by.

Hey, no judgement here. Remember my husband fucked a blond bimbo right after I buried my son, while my breasts were still swollen and sore from the milk my child would never drink.

I figured it was my right to fuck whomever I wanted to fuck until the end of time.

Anyway, that morning, the first morning of Eartha being in our house—or next to us in our garden house—I woke up with a headache. I stumbled into the bathroom, downed a painkiller, took a shower, then put on sweats. I looked out the window and saw the garden house. "Shit." I had nearly forgotten that some little hippy dudette was staying there. Last night I had made Hayword swear he would not leave me alone with her. But he was gone.

I texted him, "You better get your ass back here."

He texted right back, "I'm having my police source check her out. Chill. We've still got one great thing coming to us today."

"I'll 'chill' you, buddy," I said.

I went downstairs. Violeta was working in the kitchen, cleaning up Hayword's mess, no doubt. She looked up at me and nodded. Her eyes were red. She brought me a cup of coffee and a croissant.

"I told you that you don't have to wait on me," I said. Although I liked it. I liked someone bringing me things. I liked someone cooking for me. Loved it, actually. Violeta wasn't much of a cook, but she loved us—or faked it well. It used to matter to me whether she meant it or not. Now I didn't care. I took everything at face value.

It was much easier that way.

Okay, maybe not everything at face value. But Violeta, at least.

I drank the coffee—gulped it—and pulled flakes of dough off of the croissant and let them melt in my mouth.

I squinted and looked over at Violeta who was putting dishes into the dishwasher.

"How are you this morning, Violeta?"

She shrugged. "Do you want to know?"

I raised an eyebrow. Did I want to know? Hmmm. Well, hell, I had asked the question. I couldn't get out of it now.

"Yes, of course I want to know."

"*Mi madre* is dying," she said. "My sister said it'll be any time now."

Seemed like Violeta's mother had been dying for about ten years now. Or had she already died? I bit my tongue so that I didn't say that out loud. Violeta probably just wanted to go home early. Or take some time off. But she wouldn't lie about a thing like that, would she?

No. I would. I had. Once when I stood up one of my love nesters, I told him a relative had died and I had to go out of town unexpectedly. A place where they didn't have phones. I gave myself points that I picked a relative who was actually dead.

"Shouldn't you go home then?" I said to Violeta. See, this was why everyone who worked for us loved us. (Or pretended they did.) We always did right by them. "Be with your family. We'll be fine."

She shook her head. "She's in Mexico City," she said. "I can't afford to fly there."

She couldn't afford to fly to see her dying mother? That implied we were not paying her a decent living, didn't it?

"I'll buy you a ticket," I said. Hayword would love it. Helping the help always made him feel like we were one of the little people again.

"No," she said, shaking her head. "I couldn't leave you now."

"Why not now?" I had already gotten up and found my purse, had pulled out the checkbook.

"Mr. Lightman is so worried about this project," she said, "and David is having trouble at school. You've got the Benefit. The fires, the protests." She shook her head. "No. It is not a good time."

"Well, isn't it too bad your mother couldn't die on our schedule," I said. I wrote out a check for two thousand dollars. I ripped it out of the checkbook and held it out to her. "Is this enough?"

She came and looked at it but didn't take it.

"That is plenty," she said.

I set the check on the countertop.

"Mr. Lightman is always worried about some project," I said. "And David will survive." I had no idea what trouble he was having at school, but I wasn't going to ask her. Then she would know I didn't know what was going on with my own son. "I don't do much at the Benefit except stand around and still look cute. And the fires come every year and someone is always protesting something."

"The fires are bad this year," she said. "It feels like the end of the world some days."

"We live in California," I said. "Some days it is the end of the world. Please take this money as our gift. I'm so sorry about your mother. Go and stay as long as you like."

"Do you want me to find someone to help you out while I'm gone?" Violeta asked.

I shook my head. "Naw, we'll figure it out." I'd call the agency I used whenever Violeta went on vacation. "Go on."

"I'll finish cleaning up," she said. "Thank you." She looked like she wanted to hug me or something. But she didn't. I left the room. The kitchen felt more like her domain than mine.

I took my coffee and went outside to sit by the pool. I had two hours before I was meeting Mark P.—my former plumber— down at the art studio. I needed to do some yoga—or pretend to—and shower, put on my makeup so that it didn't look like I had any on, and make my hair look natural.

I didn't feel like doing any of that right then. I sat in the lounge chair and leaned back. I wished my coffee was a gin and tonic. Or one of the martinis Eartha had made. Oh Christ. I had nearly forgotten about her again. I glanced behind me. No activity that I could discern coming from the garden house. I sighed and leaned back again.

It would be so much easier if I could go to the art studio and fuck Mark P. looking like I did right now. What a relief that would be. I sighed. Who would have ever guessed that I would end up as a Hollywood wife, or an Enclave wife as we sometimes called ourselves?

Never. Never would have guessed in a million years. Hayword and I had come to California wet behind the ears, certain we were going to change the world and the movie business because we would be different from everyone else here. We didn't care about money. We didn't care what people looked like or where they came from.

We'd been in theater and we wrote this script that we thought was a play, but then we realized it would work better as a movie.

Someone knew someone who knew someone. And soon we got an offer on it. The studio loved it, loved every word, every scene. They handed us a contract and asked us how soon we could start on the rewrite.

Ah, Hollywood.

Yes, we love you, we really love you the individual you, now go get a face-lift, boob job, penile implant or whatever so you can fit in with everyone else.

Like I said, I'm not into that life much any more. Not that I don't look over the scripts Hayword writes. I do. He sends me the file and asks me to check the spelling and grammar. I agree and then I do whatever I can to make the script a bit better. I add the warmth. The humor. I make the characters real.

Although I would deny that to anyone. Even to Hayword. If he wants to believe the scripts are completely his work, let him. I could give a shit. Men's egos are so fucking fragile.

Nope. I didn't ask for this life but I got it. I'm not complaining. I let it happen, and now I've got everything.

So I am *not* complaining.

I supposed I should find out what was happening with David at school before Violeta left. Couldn't be anything too big. He loved his school. He was always texting or talking to one or more of his classmates on his phone or whatever.

I wasn't a fan of most of the new technology. I didn't even like telephones. But I used mine to make dates. Cancel dates. Never wrote anything sexually explicit or mushy on it. I wasn't an idiot.

"Wow, that was great."

I looked over my shoulder and into the sun. I put my hand up to shield my eyes. Eartha was standing there, half-dressed or half-naked, in a yoga outfit. She smiled at me.

"What was great?" I asked. Don't know why.

"Yoga," she said. "I did sun yoga out back of the garden

house. Man, it is such a cool space. Do you ever do yoga back there?"

"No, we've got a yoga studio in the house," I said. I pretended to use it every morning. And every Thursday, or almost every Thursday, some of the women from the Enclave came over and we all did yoga together. Or our version of yoga: We drank, smoked some weed, lamented our lost youth and sagging breasts.

"Oh, it's so much better outside," she said. "You can really feel the energies of the Earth."

Eartha feeling the Earth. How quaint.

"Thank you for your hospitality," Eartha said. "I've got a good feeling about this place. Some good vibes. Some sadness, that's true, but good vibrations."

"So the Beach Boys would be happy here," I said.

"Yep," she said without hesitation.

Almost no one got my ironic sardonic hysterically funny sense of humor. Points for Eartha.

"How are you this morning?" she asked. She moved around to the front of me, so I wasn't staring into the sun.

"It's a little chaotic today," I said.

Not for me but for everyone else.

My phone vibrated. I looked at it. Hayword texted, "Philip checked out Eartha. She's clean as a whistle."

"Anything I can do?" Eartha asked.

I couldn't smell anything wafting off of her today. Perhaps she had had a shower.

"You can't cook, can you?" I asked.

"Yep," she said. "Cooked for a while in New Orleans. Then at a natural foods restaurant in Santa Cruz for a time. Then at a retreat center in Oregon."

I held up my hand. "I don't need your resume," I said. "Our housekeeper has a family emergency and I have to run down to the village. I'm not sure I'll be back by dinner. I can get some takeout, but you could earn your room and board for the night by making us dinner."

"Oh," Eartha said. "I didn't know I'd get board. I like that. You need a cook, I'm it. Must be divine inspiration that I ended up on your doorstep."

"How *did* you end up on our doorstep?" I asked. "Is this some kind of real life *All About Eve?* You've been waiting in the wings to take over our lives?"

Eartha sat in the chair across from me—on the edge of it—and looked at me. She shook her head. "What's *All About Eve?*"

"The movie," I said. "You know, Ann Baxter is Eve and she is a fan of Betty Davis who is a famous theater actor. Eventually she takes over Betty Davis's life."

Eartha shrugged. "I don't watch movies."

"You don't watch movies? Well, you've had to be on this Earth a while. You've heard the line, 'fasten your seat belts; it's gonna be a bumpy ride.' That's from *All About Eve.*"

Eartha stared at me. Then she started laughing.

"I'm yanking your chain," she said. "Yes, I know that movie. I love movies. I loved that movie. But you're not an actor, right? And neither am I. What about your life would I want to take over?"

"Any part of it," I said. "I've got a pretty nice fucking life."

I kind of liked that she had tried to fool me. Didn't know why. Maybe because I figured it meant she was a little deeper than she appeared to be. Or a little meaner.

Just then Violeta came hurrying out of the house. "There's an emergency over at Mrs. Joan's place. Someone there called and asked for you to come right over."

"Me?" I said. I put my coffee cup on the table and got up. "If there's an emergency, they should call 911."

Violeta shook her head. "They said you should come right away."

"Oh Christ," I said. "All right, all right. Violeta, this is Eartha."

The two women nodded at each other.

"Eartha's gonna cook for us tonight," I said. "Could you show her around before you leave? And Eartha, if I'm not back right away, don't steal the silver. We've got your fingerprints and Hayword already had them and your name run through a database. Yeah, he's got a friend on the police force. Just like in the movies. Can't think of any particular movie."

"*Rear Window,*" Eartha said. "Jimmy Stewart's character had a friend on the police force."

"Yes, and look how well that turned out for the bad guy," I said.

Violeta stared at me. Eartha laughed.

I hurried past them and went through the house to our front door. I opened it.

Mark P. was standing on my front steps.

"What the?" I said. I quickly closed the door behind me.

"Hello, Mrs. Lightman," Mark said loudly. "Mrs. Donning sent me over to get you." He looked around. I grabbed his arm and pulled him over behind one of our bushes.

"What are you doing here?" I asked.

He was dressed in a T-shirt and jeans, a tool-belt hung from his hips, and his short black hair fell down across his forehead. I summed up the clues: He was working.

"I'm working for Mrs. Donning," he said. "I think she's crazy. She's got her toe stuck in the faucet and she's completely naked. I was downstairs working on the bathroom and she called me upstairs to help her. She is completely naked."

"You said that twice," I said.

He looked almost panicked, which was not Mark's style. He

was always cool and collected. Well, almost always. Sometimes when we were naked together, he was definitely hot.

"And she has her hands on herself in all sorts of places I don't want to see," he said.

I almost started laughing.

No need for us to hide in the bushes.

"Okay, well, I gotta see this," I said. "Take me to the spectacle."

We crossed the street and walked down the tree-lined road a bit, then went up a steep drive. I was surprised Mark P. hadn't driven over to get me. Everyone around here drove everywhere, even if it was only a block away.

"Why'd you call me?" I asked before I opened the front door to the Donning house.

"She told me to call you," he said. "She said you would understand. She didn't even want her housekeeper to know."

The door opened and Joan's housekeeper Beatriz was standing there. Mark and I hurried inside.

I smiled at Beatriz and said, "I'm going up to see the missus."

Beatriz gave Mark a dirty look and then walked away from us and went into the kitchen.

"I'll finish working on the bathroom," he said.

I looked at him. "You gonna be done in time?" I asked. "Unless this whole thing has turned you off women."

"I haven't decided yet," he said. He grinned and reached for me.

I moved away from him and hurried up the stairs. When I got to the top of them, I called out, "Joanie, I'm coming in."

I walked into the master bedroom and went to the partially closed bathroom door and pushed it open.

I had to laugh. So I did. Joan Donning was lying naked, smoking a cigarette, in her very large white recessed bathtub.

Her short black hair was slicked back, and she had on all of her makeup. Her breasts had not slipped to either side of her chest like mine would have if I were in her position. They were pointing at the ceiling, lined up together like two little soldiers waiting for orders.

"Why isn't there any water in the tub at least?" I asked.

Joan pointed to her feet. One of her toes was in the faucet.

"Have you tried turning on the water?" I asked. "Maybe the pressure would push your toe out?"

"It hurts when I do that."

I went to the window and opened it. "Gawd, Joanie. How can you stand all that smoke?"

"Can you bring me a towel at least?" she asked.

I grabbed a plush red towel from the pile near the towel heater. I unfolded it and draped it over her.

"You look even more strange now," I said.

"Do you want me to ring for coffee?" Joan asked. "Or some breakfast."

I laughed. "Joanie, why did you call me and what is going on?"

She stubbed the cigarette out on the side of the bathtub. The ashes fell into the tub with her. Then she looked around for an ashtray or something to put the stub in. Not seeing anything, she tossed it in the general direction of a small metal trash can in the corner. She missed.

"Ah, Beatriz will get it later," she said. "What do you think I was doing? I knew Mark was coming over today. I didn't really need any work, but I saw him when he came over to fix your plumbing. He looked so scrumptious. You've got your love nest. I figured I could have mine."

"I don't have a love nest," I said. "I have an art studio."

"Art studio?" she said. "Hah! We all call it the fuck studio. Like we call you Fucking Brooke. How do you do it?"

"But the plumber?" I said, ignoring her question. I was actually feeling her out—so to speak—to figure out if she knew Mark and I were lovers. Or fuckers. Whatever you call two people who occasionally copulate.

"When did you get so snobby?" she asked. "Didn't you fuck a preacher one year?"

"One summer," I said. "But that's beside the point. I'm not you. You're the one who told me you'd never even date someone who made less than a million dollars a year. And you're married to a billionaire. Mark doesn't make that much."

"I don't care about how much money he makes!" she said. "I want to fuck him, not spend him."

I looked at her.

"And Bernie is not a billionaire," she said. "And he's as flaccid as a ripe banana."

I groaned. "Thank you for that image."

"Come on," Joan said. "I'm a young woman. When I was younger, he came so quick he barely had time to insert his penis into my vagina. That wasn't much fun. And now he's too flaccid to get it into my vagina."

"I may never have sex again," I said.

"What about Hayword?" she asked. "Does he still have the wood, or is that why you go outside and play?"

"I'm not going to talk about my husband's sexual prowess," I said. "Or about my sex life at all."

"You should be careful with him," Joan said. "Katie Williams has been trying to fuck him for years. She's told me. She thinks he's a saint for putting up with you. Apparently Ken does not satisfy all of her needs despite the fact that they look like Ken and Barbie dolls together."

"Well, I wish her good luck," I said.

Joan sighed. "The only reason I volunteer to do these benefits is because I keep hoping I'll find someone to fuck," she said. "But the waiters are all so young. They don't give me a second look."

I shrugged. "Flash some green," I said. "I'm sure they'd give you a second look."

"I'm not a prostitute," she said.

"No, that would make you the John. Or the Jill."

She actually had tears in her eyes. The last time I had seen her cry was. . . . Well, I had never seen her cry.

She obviously was not going to tell me why she had brought me here. Maybe on some level she considered us friends.

I went to the medicine cabinet and opened it, found a jar of petroleum jelly. I took it over to the tub, knelt on the floor, then took a gob out and began smearing it on her big toe as far up as I could.

"Mark said you were touching yourself," I said. "What was that all about?"

"Wow," she said. "That feels nice. Could you rub my whole body in that?"

"Don't be gross," I said.

"I had heard that men like to watch women doing it," she said. "You know, to ourselves. So that's what I was doing. Only I got a little carried away and that's when my toe got stuck and I kind of forgot about Mark."

I hung my head and laughed. "I thought I had a fucked up life."

"You? You have a perfect life. And what I experienced in this bathtub was the best sex I've had in years."

"If I cared," I said, "that would be incredibly sad. Now move your foot around and see if your toe will come out."

"I can't," she said. "I've been here so long I've got a cramp. You do it."

I sighed, took a hold of her heel, and gently moved her foot back and forth.

Still stuck.

"What if it's swelling?" she said. "What if they have to cut off my toe? I should get dressed so that no one sees me like this."

"Let me get some WD-40."

"What's that?"

"Oil. I'll be right back," I said. I got up and left the bathroom and hurried out of the master bedroom and down to the first floor bathroom where Mark was working. He stood up from the toilet.

"There's nothing wrong with this toilet or any other part of the bathroom." He looked disgusted. "I could have been on a really big job today."

I didn't have time for his plumber's angst.

"You got any WD-40?" I asked.

He pulled a can out of his big ass belt and held it out to me.

"You just happen to have it on you?"

"Um, yeah," he said. "Half my work involves WD-40. No, more than half. Eighty percent. Hell, if you count today, maybe ninety-eight percent of my on the job problems could be fixed with WD-40."

Oh my gawd. How much longer was he going to talk about WD-40?

I took the can from him.

"Do you know how to use it?" he asked.

"Yeah, don't I just pucker up and blow?"

He looked at me. "No. You put that little tube where you want the oil to go and then you hit this button."

Obviously not a movie connoisseur. At least not this morning. He usually got my sense of humor.

I didn't really care if he did or didn't get my humor. He fucked like he wasn't a movie star. Which was a good thing. Movie stars fucked like they were masturbating. Cared more about how they looked and how they were coming and going than anything else.

At least that had been my limited experience.

Movie execs were fast and furious.

Writers inventive and insecure.

Politicians? Please. Impotent.

Directors. Hmmm. Sometimes too instructive.

Regular actors were too varied to categorize.

Although, really, I tried to fuck outside the business. Felt too incestuous or something otherwise.

Plumbers, electricians, teachers, restaurant owners. Male, female. I didn't care. As long as they didn't care, except for the short time we were together.

Not that I was promiscuous. That sounded like I was fucking everyone in sight. Not at all. *Not at all.* I was fairly monogamous until it was over.

Oh Christ. I was staring at Mark and imagining him naked while Joan had her toe stuck up her . . . faucet.

I hurried away, went up the stairs, and back into the master bedroom.

"Where have you been?" Joan asked. "I think my foot is about to fall off."

"Good," I said. "Then this will be over."

I got on my knees. I raised the little tubing on the can of WD-40. Then I tried to put it up the faucet, near her toe. I was at the wrong angle. I went to the other side of the bathtub. Still wrong.

"Maybe if I do it upside down," I said. I tried that. Pushed the button. Heard something, but nothing came out of the can.

"I think you need to shake it," Joan said.

I shook it.

"Now try," she said. "You better hurry. I'm getting horny again. And you're looking good this morning. Although you don't have any makeup on. What's up with that?"

Oh crap. *I didn't have on any makeup.* I was dressed in sweats. And Mark had seen me. That was it. I couldn't fuck him ever again.

"Don't look so distressed," Joan said. "You look good for someone who hasn't had any plastic surgery."

"Will you shut the fuck up," I said. "I'm trying to get you out of this mess. I can't find the right angle. I need to be closer to the faucet."

Shit. I was going to have to get into the bathtub with Joan.

"No one is allowed in my bathtub with their clothes on."

"Joanie, move your left leg over to the right. But keep the towel on. I don't want a view with a womb."

"All right, all right. Man, you're cranky in the morning."

She moved her leg up and over. I climbed into the bathtub. I tried to crouch between her legs and position the WD-40 so I could squirt it. The damn thing was supposed to work at any angle.

Finally I sat down, leaned over—with Joan's left leg practically pressed up against my cheek—and I squirted the oil up between her big toe and the faucet.

"That feels nice," Joan said.

I was about to give it another squirt when the door opened. Bernie Donning stood with his hand on the knob. His mouth fell open. He looked like a deer in headlights.

I could only imagine what we looked like.

Just then Joan's toe slipped out of the faucet and her foot fell down, knocking me back into her, so that she was kind of straddling me backwards.

"Much better." Joan.

"Good." Me.

"May I join you?" Bernie.

We both looked at him.

I didn't think he was joking.

We both started laughing.

Bernie closed the door, with him on the other side of it.

I pushed myself up off of Joan and got out of the tub. I held my hand out to her.

"I guess Bernie is a little lonely himself," I said.

Joan took my hand and I pulled her up. She got out of the tub, wrapped the towel around herself, and then looked down at her toe.

"It's a little sore," she said. "But I'll live."

I picked up the cigarette stub and put it in the trash. Not sure why I did that.

"You won't tell anyone, will you?" she asked. She put her arms around me and hugged me tightly. I could feel her hard breasts squishing up next to my . . . lower breasts. "You're the only one in this whole place I can trust. You understand life. You've had shit happen to you. The rest of these women are a bunch of bimbos."

Including you.

"We're all a bunch of bimbos," I said. "Amazon bimbos." She still held on to me.

"Sometimes I'm just so sad," she said.

I gently pulled away from her. Sadness is contagious, you know.

"Meaningless sex isn't going to make your sadness any better," I said.

Wasn't sure where that had come from. Meaningless sex was a way to pass the time.

"Then I'll make it meaningful by having a really good time."

She smiled. The tears were vanquished. She checked her makeup in the mirror. "All right. I've given you enough thrills for today. I better get dressed. I'm sure you have things to do."

I slapped her on her towel covered ass. Then I left the bathroom. Beatriz was standing in the bedroom.

I looked at her. "Where's Mr. Donning?" I asked.

"He went back downstairs," she whispered. "I told him there were cookies. She does this kind of thing for attention sometimes, you know."

We walked out of the bedroom and into the hall.

No, I didn't know and I didn't want to know.

"And her wanting attention from that boy," Beatriz said. She made a face. "She would look so foolish."

I glanced at her. Did she know about Mark and me?

"He's hardly a boy," I said. "And—"

She looked at me as we walked down the steps.

"Never mind," I said. "I'm glad everything worked out."

At the bottom of the steps, Beatriz went toward the kitchen while I went out the front door. I walked down the long curving drive. When I was almost at the end, I saw Mark's truck. He was leaning against it, his arms crossed over his tight white T-shirt. He shook his head when he saw me.

"You went running," I said.

"No, I finished my work," he said. "I always finish my work. Not that there was much to do. Some days it's tough. You have no idea how many of these old women come on to me."

I stopped about five feet from him. I had to stay at least this far away. Otherwise I'd want to touch him.

"I can imagine," I said.

"Don't give me that look," he said. "You're nothing like them. And I went after you."

"Makes me sound like I was prey and you were the predator," I said.

It didn't really sound that way. And it didn't feel that way. But I was so used to stroking men's egos that I did it without thinking.

He reached a hand out toward me. Apparently he didn't notice or care that I was dressed in sweats and hadn't put on any makeup. I guess I could fuck him again.

When I didn't move toward him, he dropped his arm to his side.

"You want to pick up lunch for us?" I asked.

"I could make you something," he said. "I make the best omelettes. I used to want to be a chef, you know, before I went into the family business."

I smiled. "I don't want you to cook for me, Mark; I want you to fuck me."

"I can do both."

I laughed.

"Isn't the way to a woman's heart through her stomach?" Mark asked.

I shook my head. "For one thing, I don't have a heart, so there's no sense searching for it. For another, I can cook, sort of. Violeta can cook, sort of. This new homeless person Hayword has brought into our house can cook. But none of them can fuck me like you can."

I walked toward the road and let my hand lightly touch his T-shirt near his belly as I walked past.

THREE

I hurried toward my house. In fact, I pretended I was jogging in case anyone saw me.

I jogged right through the open front door and into the house.

Eartha was in the kitchen, looking completely at home, chopping up vegetables at the counter. She looked up and smiled when I came in.

"You look refreshed," she said.

I really didn't want her remarking upon my appearance. Or anything else about me.

I was having second and third thoughts about her staying in our garden house and cooking for us. What had I been thinking?

"There's plenty of food in the house," she said. "I've got a great dinner planned for you."

"It doesn't have to be great," I said. "Fair to middling will work for us. I've got to go into the village."

"To your studio?" she asked.

I squinted at her. How did she know about my studio?

"Violeta was giving me the schedule for the day," Eartha said. "She told me you work at your art studio for part of the day. I'd love to see some of your work. I've dabbled in art some myself."

I leaned against the refrigerator and folded my arms across my chest.

"Where you from anyway?" I asked.

She looked back down at her vegetables. "Everywhere. Nowhere. Most of my family is gone now. So I wander the world and find community wherever I go."

"You do this all the time?" I asked. "Like with us? You find people and you stay with them?"

She nodded. "Sure. People are so bereft of real connection and community that they almost always welcome me."

"We're not bereft of anything," I said.

"Oh, not you," she said. She looked up. "You have everything. At least I would imagine you do. Although we don't ever know what's going on in another person's heart. Or in their home, do we? By the way, the house phone rang so I answered it. I hope that was all right. It was your husband. He wanted you to pick up David after school."

"Oh Christ," I said.

I hurried out back and got my phone from my chair by the pool. I found a text message and voice mail.

I didn't feel like talking to Hayword this morning.

I texted that I couldn't pick up David.

The phone rang, so I answered it.

"I've got a big meeting," he said. "It's at four. I'll never be able to pick David up and get back here in time."

"I've got an appointment," I said. "I can't break it. Can't David go home with a classmate or something?"

"It's about that movie," he said.

"*Powerbreakers?*" The movie he had been rewriting for who knew how long. Time to let it go. Let them hire someone else to fix it.

"No, no," he said. He sounded breathless, excited, the way he always did when he thought everything was going to change. "*Zombie Town.*"

I groaned.

"I don't give a shit about that stupid ass movie," I said.

I was going to be late. I had to shower. I had to dress. I had to imagine Mark and me together.

"Brooke, they are ready to shoot," Hayword said. "Another studio bought it when Jack Meredith agreed to direct. Jack Meredith, Brooke! It'll be a blockbuster. And they want some rewrites. They're going to pay me bonuses, give me points, and I'll be an executive producer."

Ahhh, Hayword's dream: to be a producer. What little boy or girl dreams of growing up to be a producer? They might dream of becoming a writer, maybe. A director. An actor. But a producer? I don't think so.

But Hayword wanted to be the one in charge. He still believed he could make things better. People and their talents would actually matter if he was the boss.

"This movie could change everything for us," he said.

I had heard this so many times.

"It's a fucking zombie movie," I said. "What could it change?"

"Jack Meredith mentioned you," he said. "In his e-mail to the studio head of AFT."

AFT? That was a decent studio. They did some artsy movies and some blockbusters.

"Me? Why?"

"They all remember *Love and Other Insanities,*" he said. "They liked the human touch you brought to the characters."

"That's because they were human," I said. "Zombies are not. Zombies are so stupid. Who could be interested in them? They aren't sexy. You can't fuck them. You can't have dinner with them for the same reason you can't fuck them: Parts of their bodies would be falling off into the soup or into you or else you would become dinner."

"See, there," Hayword said. "Nobody thinks like you do."

Oh no. Hayword was sucking up to me. That meant he really wanted this.

"I can't break this appointment," I said. "It's a doctor's appointment I booked months ago."

"A doctor's appointment?" His voice was suddenly different. No longer the weasely Hollywood man. It was my husband's voice. "Is something wrong?"

"No, no, I'm sure not," I said. What a fucking manipulative liar I was. Like he didn't have enough to worry about.

"No," I said. "It's nothing at all. Just a woman thing. Don't want to talk to you about it or you may never want to have sex with me again."

"Brooke, you can talk to me about anything," he said. "I'll listen."

There were so many things wrong with those two sentences. But I didn't want to talk about any of that now

"Maybe you could pick David up early," I said, "and take him with you. He loves going to the office with you."

"I'll take care of it," he said.

"All right," I said. "I'll try to be home by dinner."

"Aren't you going to wish me luck?"

"Luck? For what?"

"For my meeting," he said.

"Uh, sure," I said. "But weren't you already paid? And aren't they going to shoot it anyway?"

"Yes, I was paid," he said, "and yes, they're scheduled to

start shooting soon. But if I get on as an executive producer and then they let me doctor my own script—or you doctor it—we could make a difference. This movie could change the lives of millions of people. It could change the world."

A zombie movie? Maybe I should read the script: I didn't remember any life-changing material in it when he'd told me the story. It was life-changing for the people who got eaten by the zombies. Or those people who became zombies. But those were merely characters in a movie. It wasn't going to change the *world.*

"Maybe you should change the title to *Zombie,*" I said.

"They do want to change the title," he said. "Why *Zombie?*"

"It could be like the movie *Gandhi,*" I said, "except we're following the life of an extraordinary zombie leader who changed the world by becoming vegetarian and learning to love the living and the dead."

"Man, I love the way your mind works," he said. "Gotta go, babe. I'll pick up David." He hung up.

I looked at the phone. "I was kidding," I said. "I was being a sarcastic bitch."

It was no fun when he didn't notice.

My hangover was beginning to dissipate, or I was beginning to dissipate. In any case, I was hungry. I needed to eat before I went down to the village. Damn. And Violeta was gone.

I went into the house and up the back stairs so I wouldn't have to see Eartha. I took a shower—man, that felt good—and then I put on my makeup and stood in my very large closet wondering what I should wear.

Mark had just seen me in sweats. He obviously didn't care what I wore. Or else he was too polite to say anything.

I put on a black camisole, a sheer blue blouse, and tight black jeans. No. Tight black jeans would leave creases. I pulled them off and put on a tight pair of black slacks made of something unnatural. No creases.

Then I stared at myself in the mirror. I was acting as though I cared what Mark P. thought about me. I didn't. He should care what I thought about him.

I looked at the clock. Another hour before I had to be there. I could pick up something to eat for us, or I could let Mark make me an omelette. No. That was too domestic. Didn't want set any precedent with that.

Oh crap. I would have to leave Eartha in the house alone. I couldn't do that. Okay. Wait. I could lock up the house so she would only be able to get into the garden house while I was gone. Wait. That wouldn't work. How could she make dinner if she was in the garden house? Perhaps that particular ship had sailed. We'd go out for dinner. Or I'd pick up a pizza.

I was not leaving her in this house. She could be waiting until we all left to call her accomplices. Burglars could come in and strip a house clean in a very short time.

I texted Hayword, "I have to leave, but I can't leave Eartha in the house."

He texted back almost immediately. "I told you that Philip thoroughly vetted her. She's fine. Besides Violeta is there."

"Violeta had to leave. Something about her mother. Maybe Eartha's such a good criminal that she never leaves any evidence behind during her crime sprees."

No answer from Hayword. I waited. Nothing. Was this his passive aggressive way of saying, "Shut the fuck up?"

I went downstairs. Eartha was still in the kitchen. I glanced over at the table. One place setting. With a bowl of something on the table.

"I made you a little salad," Eartha said. "Violeta said you'd only had a croissant for breakfast. And coffee."

"It's how the French eat," I said. "And they seem to do all

right." I didn't like Violeta talking about me to strangers.

"You don't have to eat it," Eartha said. "You don't want it, I'll eat it."

I walked over to the table, pulled out the chair, and sat in it. I looked down at the bowl. It was filled with green leafy stuff. With specks of something salmon-colored throughout.

"What is that?" I asked.

Eartha came over and looked where I was pointing.

"Salmon," she said.

"Oh."

Some rice. Or else maggots. Wasn't sure. Bits of olive. Something red.

"What's that?" I asked, pointing.

"Radicchio," she said. "And that's spinach, dandelion greens. It was all in your refrigerator."

"I don't know why," I said. "I don't let Violeta make salads, except for David. He's gotten a little pudgy this year. But Hayword doesn't like anything green. He likes meat and potatoes. Reminds him of home."

"You're in California," Eartha said.

"So?"

"You can get anything fresh here," Eartha said. "Fresh salmon. Fresh greens. Fresh pasta. Fresh cheese. Fresh whatever."

"We're not a very fresh family," I said. "We're a little stale, and we like our food that way."

Eartha shrugged. "I'll eat it."

I held up my hand.

"I'll try it," I said. I dug the fork in, speared a bunch of stuff, put it into my mouth, and then chewed.

My eyes widened. How could rabbit food taste this good? I know, calling a salad rabbit food is a cliché. I actually would like to eat differently, but Violeta knows how to cook food with lard. Getting her not to use lard had been such an effort. As least as far as I was concerned. I couldn't teach her California cuisine. Or any kind of cuisine. I remembered how we had eaten when I was a kid. Meat, starch, and canned vegetables. Not that we had canned vegetables now, but vegetables weren't the highlight of our meals.

Okay. If I was really honest, I'd have to say I don't really pay much attention to what I eat, or what any of us eats. I make sure there's enough food in the house—I make sure Violeta makes sure there's enough food in the house. Beyond that, who cares? It's just . . . food.

"What kind of dressing is that?" I asked. "It makes everything melt in my mouth."

I suddenly felt starved. I kept eating the salad and talking.

"I added some avocado to a basic vinaigrette," Eartha said, "along with a few herbs and spices. Found a can of black beans and I added some to the salad. Be better if they were fresh beans, or at least dried beans freshly soaked and cooked."

The dish was almost as good as the martini she had made last night.

I finished every bit of it.

I wanted to lick the bowl.

"Is that your one great thing for today?" I asked, pushing the bowl away from me.

"I don't know," she said. "That's up to you."

I squinted as I looked at her. "This isn't like *The Cook* is it?"

"I don't know that movie," she said.

"It's a book," I said. "In it a cook comes to work for this very fucked up family. He makes the most amazing meals that satisfy each and every family member. They feel so obligated to him and so dependent upon him that soon they are all waiting on him and he's the boss of everything."

Eartha laughed. "I'm not sure I've ever met anyone as suspicious as you, although the suspicion seems to come and go."

"Look, I've got to leave now," I said. "I can drop you off in the village and then pick you up when I'm done."

I didn't know what else to do. I wasn't stupid enough to leave a complete stranger in my house all afternoon. I'd have to cut my time with Mark short, but that was the way it was.

"Sure," Eartha said. "Be nice to check out the village. Go to the library."

"Don't count on the library," I said. "It's barely open nowadays. None of them are. But you can buy liquor and semi-automatics 24/7. Gotta love California."

I brushed my teeth. By the time I came downstairs again, Eartha had tidied up the kitchen. She smiled at me and followed me outside. She seemed a bit subdued today. Yesterday I thought we had let a latter-day wild child into our midst. Today she seemed to have slipped easily into the role of a domestic.

What kind of game was she playing?

We got into my little maroon sports car. (I'm not telling you what kind of car. I don't intend to advertise for anyone or anything. This is my life. It ain't sponsored by nothing or nobody.) I put the top down, and we drove slowly down the winding road. Eartha stared up at the sky and the tall trees and bushes on either side of the road.

Today I smelled no smoke, and the winds seemed to have quieted down.

"You must love living here," Eartha said. "It's quite beautiful. You can feel like you're in nature out here even though you're in a community. Some beautiful trees and flowers."

I kept my eyes on the road. There was always some asshole driving these curves too fast. And half the people coming up this canyon road were all liquored up.

"I don't notice the fauna and flora," I said. "I don't leave my yard much, except to go to the studio. There are some trails down by my art studio, but I don't use them."

"Really?" Earth said. "I would imagine the three of you go out hiking all the time."

"Imagine all you want," I said, "but we don't get out much. Hayword is always working. David's always on the computer or some gadget and I'm always—"

Out of the corner of my eye, I could see her looking at me.

"You're always what?" she asked.

"Nothing," I said. "I'm always doing nothing." Drinking a little. Watching television. Making dates. Planning benefits. Only I didn't do that much planning. I did show up though. Always in the sexiest dress. I had that reputation. I liked having that reputation. Since I was from the Midwest, they thought I'd be all nice and full of cornball humor without any fashion taste. I liked to prove them all wrong.

Not that I had any fashion taste. I could give a shit. Really. I would wear my sweats all day long if I could. If I never had to see any people, that was probably what I would do. Although David and Hayword got a little concerned if I walked around in my pajamas for too many days in a row.

Not that I did that often. Probably once or twice a year. Went to a therapist for it once, when Hayword said he couldn't stand watching me drink and drug my life away (like I couldn't stand to watch him whore his life away as a Hollywood dickwad). The therapist concluded I got depressed twice a year on Alberto's birth date and death date. She said this to me as if it were a great revelation.

"No fucking shit, Sherlock," I told her. "You charge three hundred dollars an hour for that hunk of wisdom? For that kind of money, you better be going down on me."

Needless to say, I didn't go back to see her.

"I find time in Nature quite sustaining," Eartha said. "Do you want to go on a walk with me sometime? We could go on one of the trails near your studio."

I glanced at her. That sounded like she was going to stay for a while.

"I'll see if I can work it into my calendar," I said.

Eventually the road straightened, and we were headed for the village. At one vantage point, we were up above the ocean. I could see smoke billowing from some canyon or cliff side in the distance. More than one smoke column actually. I wondered if Hayword had encountered any trouble getting to Los Angeles.

Then the view disappeared and we were in the village. I drove slowly down the main road and passed by most of the touristy shops.

"The library is down there," I said, pointing. "How about I meet you on this corner in two hours."

"Sure," Eartha said. "Can I see your art studio first?"

"No," I said. "Nobody goes there. Hayword barely knows where it is. You got a phone?"

Eartha shook her head. "I believe in face to face communication. Who knows what all those waves are doing to our brains?"

"They're turning us all into zombies," I said. I leaned over and opened the glove compartment. I reached in, found something slick and hard, and pulled it out.

"Here's a throwaway," I said. I glanced at the number I'd taped to it. "Five." That was the speed dial number. "David is always losing his phone, so I've got extras. My number is on the speed dial." I showed her. "Right there. Number one. In case we can't find one another."

She nodded. "You want me to pick up anything for the house?"

Someone behind me honked. He was way too close to my car. He was so close to my bumper I could see the veins in his forehead popping out. Looked like he had eggs for breakfast, judging from his teeth. I motioned for him to go around. He inched closer.

"Hey!" I yelled. "I don't know you well enough for you to be that far up my ass!"

He couldn't hear me, but Eartha got an earful. "Fucking asshole. Like it's gonna ruin his day to wait two goddamned minutes. No, Eartha, I don't need anything."

Eartha got out of the car. She crossed the street and kept walking. I drove away quickly.

I took a circuitous route to the studio in case I was being followed. I wasn't paranoid, much, but I didn't want anyone I knew to know where the studio was. The only people who ever came there were people I fucked. Period.

Oh, and the cleaning lady.

I pressed the garage door opener and drove the car inside. Closed the door again. I nearly always used the garage so that no one would know if I was there or not. And my paramours always parked a few blocks over and then walked up.

I didn't know a single neighbor.

Hadn't a clue what they thought about me. But I kept the lawn mowed, and I was quiet, so they probably had no thought about me, which was fine by me.

I got out of the car, unlocked the side door, and went inside the house. It was cool and dark and felt empty, even though I'd been there a few days earlier. Sometimes I thought about getting a cat so that the house would feel lived in. But then I worried I might forget about the cat, and it would die, and I would never be able to get the stink out.

I went into the bedroom. The bed was made. The room had been aired out. Good. The cleaning lady had been here. Or was she the maid? What was the difference? I was never clear. All of my neighbors in the Enclave had maids and/or housekeepers.

I heard a tap on the window of my back door. I walked through the tiny kitchen and opened the door. Mark P. stood there, grinning, holding a bag of groceries.

"Hey, you," he said. He came in and kissed me on the mouth.

He quickly put away the groceries while I watched. Then he put his hands on my waist and pulled me toward him.

"I haven't been able to stop thinking about you," he said.

"I can feel that," I said.

"You looked so sexy," he said. "Straight out of bed. No makeup. Hardly any clothes. Oh man. Take it off."

"My clothes?" I said.

"No," he said. "Well, yes, but take off your makeup. I want to see you natural again. Take off your clothes. All of them. You always leave your bra on when we make love."

We walked toward the bedroom, holding onto one another.

"Mark, I don't like anyone telling me what to do."

"I'm not telling," he said. "I'm asking."

I shrugged. "Okay." I went into the bathroom and shut the door. I leaned close to the mirror and pulled off my fake eyelashes. I washed my face with soap, then looked in the mirror. I looked like a drag queen who had been crying. I turned on the shower and got in. I tried to keep the water away from my hair, but I scrubbed my face again.

Then I got out and rubbed myself dry with a towel. I glanced in the mirror. "Oh geez," I said. "Ah well. This is me."

Maybe seeing me like this would scare Mark off. Probably about time to end it anyway.

I let the towel drop, and I opened the door.

Mark was lying on top of the covers naked.

"Fuck," he said. "You are beautiful."

He was fucking blind.

He pulled down the covers, and I got into bed. I could see he was ready to rumble.

"I'm not ready yet," I whispered.

He smiled. Then he went down on me.

I was soon ready.

Very ready.

"It's gonna be fast and hard," he said.

I laughed. "Okay by me," I said.

He put on a condom and then he was fast and hard. We came almost in the same instant.

Geez fucking Louise.

"Wow," I said when we moved apart. "That was fun. Let's do it again."

"Give a man a chance," he said, lying on his back.

I straddled him. I ran my fingers over his nipples and leaned over and kissed his ear. "I'm sure it won't take long," I said.

He grinned. I lay down next to him, and he turned on his side to face me.

"Now tell me that wasn't the best sex you've ever had," he said.

"It didn't last long enough for it to be the best sex I've ever had," I said. "But it was good."

"We should be together," he said. "We're so good together."

"We have good sex together," I said. "Besides that, we don't know if we'd be good or not."

I turned away from him. I didn't want to have this conversation again. It was usually at this point in my affairs that I'd break it off—when they got too needy—but I liked Mark. I was not finished with him or his body.

He curled up behind me and put his arms around me.

"We'd be great together," he said.

"The sex never stays this good," I said. "How long were you married?"

He'd told me, but I didn't remember.

"Four years," he said, "and the sex was never as good as this."

"Sex is the least of any long-term relationship," I said.

I could feel him getting hard up against me again.

"Although it is the most of our relationship," I said

He moved a little away from me, so I couldn't feel his hard-on. I turned around and smiled at him.

"I don't like it when you talk to me like I'm some fucking kid," he said. "We're only a few years apart in age. You're not some relationship sage. If you were, you wouldn't be down here fucking me."

"Right at this moment I'm not fucking anyone," I said.

I suddenly felt like a salesman: *What can I do for you today that'll put you into my vagina?*

"Do you still fuck Hayword?" he asked.

I flinched a bit. Didn't like him saying Hayword's name.

"Of course I do," I said. I felt naked. I wanted to put on my clothes. Some makeup. Have a fucking drink.

"Does he wear a condom?"

"Yes, he does," I said. I rolled over and got out of bed.

Mark reached for my hand. I tried to get away, but he was quicker than I was. He pulled me back onto the bed.

"He does?" Mark asked. "But you're married. Does he cheat on you?"

"He did," I said. "Once. At least as far as I know. I told him I'd kill him if he did it again."

"Was it a long time ago?"

"I don't want to talk about this." I lay back. Mark kissed my mouth.

"I want to know you," he said.

"You know me," I said. "I want to fuck or I want to leave. I don't have much time today."

I was trying to make him mad so that he'd stop talking.

Weren't men supposed to be so stifled in their emotions that they never wanted to talk?

Today Mark was a regular Chatty Cathy.

"I don't have sex with anyone else," he said. "Haven't since we started."

"I appreciate that," I said, "but you don't have to do that on my account."

"Why did he cheat on you?"

"What kind of question is that?" I said. "That sounds like you're blaming me."

"I'm not blaming you," he said. "I was wondering how anyone could cheat on you. You're smart, you're beautiful, I bet you're talented at more than just fucking."

"I never asked him why," I said. "My baby boy had just died, so I didn't care why. I was about to lose my mind and then I walked in on him fucking this blond bimbo. I mean I can still see it. They were standing up. He'd never fucked me standing up. And his pants were around his ankles. His shirt was still on. I could see his ass, could see him pushing himself up into this woman. And I'd just buried my child. *We* had just buried our child. Our baby boy. I couldn't be alone with the kids any more. David was two and he cried all the time, and Fern was becoming a teen and she hated me, blamed me for everything wrong in the whole fucking world. So I went to his office. I could see this woman's blond hair and huge bare breasts. Her huge bare *fake* breasts. And her mouth was slack. Couldn't see her eyes, but her mouth was slack. Like she was some kind of animal being fucked, like she didn't know we had just buried our child. But he knew. He knew. If I had had a gun that day, I would have killed them both."

I stopped. I couldn't believe I had said any of that out loud. *Fuck, fuck, fuck.*

I sat up. I wanted my clothes. I was too fucking naked.

I didn't want to see Mark's face. Didn't want to see the pity. *Crap, crap, crap.*

Now I was a human being to him. A human being with problems.

No, a human being with a past. That was all.

"Can I ask how he died?"

"Sudden infant death syndrome," I said. "He was eight months old."

"I'm sorry," he said. "I had no idea."

"Just forget I told you," I said. I grabbed his shirt that was still on the end of the bed and put it on. There, that felt better.

"I'm glad you told me," he said. "It makes me love you more."

Oh fuck.

"Mark," I said. "Don't say that. Don't feel that. We are ships passing in the night and occasionally bumping up against one another."

He laughed. "You know, Brooke, I can love you without wanting anything from you. I'm perfectly happy with the way things are." He shrugged. "Maybe not perfectly happy but happy. Now wipe that look of terror off your face—you remind me of me when I saw Mrs. Donning in the tub this morning. I'll make you something to eat or we can make love again."

"I don't want to make love again," I said. "But I would be obliged if you wanted to fuck my brains out again."

Afterward, we lay in bed together. Usually I was up and outta there, but something about telling him about Alberto had knocked the stuffing out of me. I lay in his arms, half asleep. I may have even fallen to sleep a couple of times.

"I'm surprised you never got divorced," he said. "That happened to a friend of mine and his marriage didn't survive. He told me that most marriages don't survive the loss of a child."

"I wanted a divorce," I said. "I was going to take David with me and move back to Michigan or up to Oregon. I told Hayword he could keep Fern. She was terror on wheels even back then. It was as though she came out of the womb loathing me. But Hayword begged me to stay. He promised it would get better. He swore he would never cheat again. I could have anything I wanted. I told him I wanted my son back and I wanted the image of him fucking the blond bimbo out of my brain. He couldn't accomplish either of those miracles. Not that they would be equal miracles. He could have fucked anyone he wanted if that would have brought back my son. But life isn't like that."

Mark had to stop asking me questions because I kept answering them.

I wasn't going to tell him that I had never talked about this to anyone before. Not even Hayword. Certainly not Hayword.

"I told him I wanted a place of my own. This place. I saw it from the outside first. Seemed peaceful. Never went out back before I bought it—just saw the yard from the windows. Then after I got the keys and it was mine, I went out back. It's got a nice big yard. Used to be a garden there. And there was a swing set. An older metal swing set like the kind I had when I was a kid."

"In the olden days," Mark said, chuckling.

"Yep, like in the olden days," I said. "Something about that swing set broke my heart. I fell to my knees right then. Bawled my eyes out. I had someone come and take it away the next day. I've hardly been out back since."

And I had hardly cried since then either.

"I remember when I got divorced," Mark said. "I know it's not the same. Not even close. But it was so sad to me, and when I returned to the house, you know, months after I'd moved out, and I went in the backyard for something and saw a new swing set and plastic playhouse. I felt completely lost. It wasn't my life any more. I had always wanted a swing in the back for my son, Ian, but we'd never gotten one. And my ex had always wanted a little playhouse for him, but I couldn't stand the idea of him playing in plastic. I kept promising to build him a fort or tree house, but I never did. At least not there. I felt bad about it all for a long time, but then I bought my own house, and I built a tree house for him."

"Wow," I said. "You handle adversity better than I do. I'm still mad about all of it."

"Yeah," he said. "It was good, except Ian fell out of the tree house. Broke his arm. That was fairly traumatic. More for us than for him."

I got up on my elbow and looked at him. "Are you making that up? He really fell out of the tree house?"

Mark nodded.

I started to laugh. I lay back and laughed and laughed.

"You have a sick sense of humor," he said.

"Now that is the truth."

I heard the phone ring. An old-fashioned ring, like a rotary phone. That was the ring tone on my emergency phone. No one was supposed to call me on that phone unless it was a true emergency.

My heart started to race. I quickly got out of bed, found my purse, and dug around in it for the right phone. My other one was off.

"Please let Davey be all right," I whispered. "Let him be all right. Let Fern be all right."

I answered it.

"Brooke?"

Hayword.

"What's wrong?" I asked. "Is everyone okay?"

"Everyone is fine," he said. "I tried you on the other phone, but I couldn't get through."

"I told you I had an appointment," I said.

I went into the bathroom and closed the door. I began putting on my clothes.

"You scared the shit out of me," I said.

"I'm sorry, Brooke," he said, "but there's been a change in plans. The studio head really wants you to be at this meeting. If you were done with the doctor, I thought you could pick up David, bring him with you, and head into the city."

"I'll never get there by four," I said. "The traffic will be a nightmare."

"They'll wait," he said. "Look, they've really got a hard-on for this movie, but they need it doctored. They want you. They want to see your take on it."

"Did you tell them I don't give a shit about some goddamn zombie movie?" I asked.

"Yes," Hayword said. "But come on. Aren't you flattered? They want you!"

"For a fucking zombie movie," I said.

"I called David's school," he said. "I said we needed to pick him up early. You could even drop him at home. Let him stay with Eartha. I promise you she'll be great with him."

"Too late to send me a driver?" I asked.

"Yes," he said. "Come on, Brooke. You can do it. It'll be painless. These guys are the real deal."

"None of those guys are the real deal," I said. "Where are you meeting?"

"Juliet's, off Wilshire," he said. "You can call me when you're about twenty minutes out."

"Like I'll know," I said. "Okay. I'll try. But don't expect me to be charming."

"I expect you to be yourself," he said.

"Don't be nice to me, Hayword," I said. "I don't respond well to that."

He laughed. "But I'm always nice to you."

"Yeah, see."

I hung up. Turned the phone off. Whatever it was they called it now. I ended transmission.

I sighed. How the fuck was I going to do this? And why was I going to do this?

So I didn't have to spill any more of my guts to Mark P.

Christ with a camera.

I went into the bedroom.

Mark had his pants on.

Too bad.

I handed him his shirt.

"Everything all right?" he asked.

I nodded. "I have to go to a meeting in L.A. My husband thinks it's an emergency. Not sure why."

Mark put his arms around me. We hugged.

"Stay and eat the food," I said. "I don't want it to go to waste."

"It'll wait," he said. "When can I see you again?"

"I'll text you," I said. We let each other go. I started to leave.

"I don't have any work for the rest of the afternoon," he said. "You want me to drive you to Los Angeles?"

I hesitated at the bedroom door. I looked at him. He smiled. That was so fucking tempting.

No, I couldn't. I still had to pick up David and Eartha, take them home.

"I know a lot of shortcuts," he said.

"There are no fucking shortcuts from here to Wilshire Boulevard."

"You'd be surprised," he said. "Plus, wouldn't you be more relaxed for your meeting if I drive."

A minute ago I was trying to figure out how to never see him again because he knew too much about me.

I looked at him. His eyebrows were raised in expectation. He still smiled. His arms were loose at his side. I crossed my arms.

"I have to pick up my son and this homeless woman staying at our house," I said.

He nodded. "I could pick you up outside your house in twenty minutes. If anyone sees us, you could say I was working at the Donning place and I offered to take you downtown. Unless you don't think anyone would believe you would ride with the help."

"Ride the help, yes," I said. "Catch a ride with the help, no."

I did not relish driving in rush hour in L.A. Not that I couldn't do it. Twenty plus years of living out here had taught me a lot about driving in California. Mostly it went like this: If you are not going at least twenty miles over the speed limit, get the fuck out of my way so I can continue to hurtle down the drive/road/ cow path/freeway past you at death-defying speeds while flipping you off and talking on the phone and eating all at the same time.

"Okay, let's do it," I said.

Mark looked speechless.

"What?" I asked. "You didn't think I'd do it?"

"Not in a million years," he said.

"Well, you can take it back," I said. "I can go by myself."

"No, I want to take you," he said. "It'll be the first time we'll be out in public."

"Public?" I said. "No, we'll be in your truck on the highway most of the time."

"What could be more public?"

"Oh Christ," I said. "I better get some sunglasses and a big floppy hat to disguise myself. Maybe wear a caftan and flip-flops. Will that do it?"

I made a face at him and then quickly left the house, got in the car in the garage, and pulled out into the driveway. I phoned

Eartha and asked her where she was. Next I called the school and told them I'd be there in a few minutes to get David. I drove to where Eartha said she'd be, and I picked her up.

"Change of plans," I said when she got into the car. "I gotta go to L.A. Can you watch David for us and make dinner? That would be two additional great things you did today."

She closed the door, and I sped down the road, heading toward David's school. *"Two* additional great things?" she asked.

"Yeah, that breakfast lunch thing you made," I said. "It was really good."

"I'm glad you liked it," she said. "Cool. Yes, I'd love to meet David and hang out with him. Maybe he can help make dinner."

"David doesn't do much in real life," I said. "He spends an inordinate amount of time on his phone. I've checked. It isn't porn. No dirty pictures. I don't know what the hell he's doing."

Eartha didn't say anything.

"I'm not an overprotective mother," I said. "I was with Fern, maybe, and now she hates my guts. I figure I'll let David be his own little man and he'll still love me."

Saying that out loud sounded pathetic.

Or maybe I hadn't had enough to eat . . . or drink yet today.

"You don't have a flask or anything on you, do you?" I asked.

"A flask?" Eartha asked. "You mean something to drink? No, I'm sorry I don't. Had some weed, but I smoked the last of it last night."

"In my garden house?" I asked.

"Yes, I figured you wouldn't mind," she said.

"You figured wrong," I said.

"I sat by the window."

"What if David had smelled it?" I said. "Or the police came by." I was grasping at straws. I really didn't give a shit that she'd smoked it. I was annoyed she didn't have any left. Or any liquor.

"I don't drink anyway," Eartha said. "The fermenting process brings out the trickster spirits of whatever plant is being fermented. That can create problems. That's how people get addicted, I believe."

"Then how did you know how to make that martini?" I said. "You must have had to taste it."

"Sure, I had to taste it. I'm not religious about not drinking or anything."

I slowed the car as we neared the school. Tall eucalyptus trees circled the building. I had gone to school in a school built in a farmer's field. We didn't have any trees. Must be nice to go to a place like this.

"Besides," she said. "There wasn't any liquor in those martinis."

"What?" I slammed on the brakes a little too hard as a kid stepped in front of me. "That's impossible."

"Nope, not a drop. But it was really good, wasn't it?"

The broad had fucking tricked me.

I wasn't sure I liked that.

Wasn't sure I disliked it either.

I could see David up on the steps waiting for me. When he saw me, he smiled and hurried toward the car. I couldn't help but smile too. David always appeared to be glad to see me. Or anyone. He was a good-natured kid. Almost every time I saw him I thought of his sister, who was not good-natured. Maybe she was to other people but not around me. Or around her father as far as I could tell. She was working on her master's degree in psychology. I couldn't imagine anyone going to her for help. They'd have to be crazy.

"Hello, love," I said when David opened the door and got into the back seat. It wasn't much of a backseat, but it would do.

"I can't believe you got me out of school early," he said. "Thanks, Mom. What are we going to do? Do you have something planned?"

I looked back at him. "It's nice to see you, too, David. Actually, you're going home with Eartha. This is Eartha. She's staying with us for a while. Violeta had to visit her sick mother."

"Oh," he said. He sounded disappointed.

"How do you do, David?" Eartha said. "I'm really glad to meet you. Maybe you'd want to help me with dinner. Or we could go outside and I could teach you some yoga."

David nodded. "Sure. Whatever."

"David, what's that in your hair?" I asked.

"What?" He felt around and touched something pink in his hair. "Ewwww!" he said. "Get it out! Get it out!"

"Stay calm," I said. "It's probably gum. Were you chewing gum last night?" I turned to Eartha. "You got any scissors in your bag?"

Eartha dug around in her purse until she came up with a small sewing kit. She opened the top of it and took out a tiny pair of scissors and handed them to me.

"Get it out!" David said. He was nearly hysterical.

"David! Stop it! It's gum. If you hold still, I'll take care of it. Lean forward." I turned around in my seat. He put his head down. I grabbed his hair where the gum was and I cut it all off.

Now he had a hole in the top of his head.

"Much better," I said. I threw the hair and gum into the trash and didn't look at Eartha as I handed the scissors back to her.

"Can I look in the mirror?" David asked.

"Naw, you can get a better look at home."

I put the car into gear and started forward. I was careful not to hit any children or the strange man lurching across the road. He was wearing a raggedy suit and he looked like he was partially covered in dirt. He walked in a daze, right into the woods and disappeared.

"I don't like the homeless getting all the way up to David's school," I said.

"No, much better if they stay out of sight in the village," Eartha said.

"Do you know him, David?" I asked. He didn't answer. I glanced in the rearview mirror. He was doing something on his phone. "David?"

"Huh?" He didn't look up.

"I asked if you knew that man?"

"What man?"

"Never mind."

I drove us back to the house. Once inside, David went straight to his room. I looked at Eartha and shrugged.

"Okay, you've got the phone with my number," I said, "or you can use the house phone. I've got a list of the speed dial numbers next to it. I'm hoping the meeting won't be long. We might go out to eat or we might come home. Do you want me to call you and let you know?"

"How about I make David a snack now and then I'll make dinner around seven. If you're home, you're home. If not, we'll eat it."

"That sounds fair," I said. I needed to run upstairs and change and put on makeup. "You know, Eartha, I'm leaving you with my most valued possession." I put my hand up. "Now before you get on your high horse and point out that a child is not a possession, I think you should know I was talking about the Ming dynasty urn I have in our bedroom."

Eartha laughed.

"Don't let anyone in," I said. "Even if they promise to do one great thing a day."

FOUR

I changed clothes quickly. Then I heard David scream. He must have looked in the mirror.

I hesitated, sighed, and then I went to his room. I knocked before I opened the door and went inside.

"Mom! What did you do? There's a hole in my head!"

"There's not a hole in your head. If there were, you'd be dead." I sat on the bed next to him.

"I wish I were dead," he said. "You know this means I walked around all day with gum in my hair and no one told me. I bet that's why Ariel Williams didn't talk to me all day."

Ariel Williams. Our neighbor's kid? I tried to remember her. Couldn't come up with a picture.

"Are you talking about Katie and Ken's daughter? From down the road?" Or up the road. Around the curve. Whatever.

"Mom," he said. "You know who she is. She's been my girlfriend forever."

"Forever is a long time," I said. "Does she know she's your

girlfriend? I mean, this isn't one of those things where you stare into her window at night while she's asleep and then you claim she's your girlfriend?"

"No!" he said. "And she'll be at the benefit party. I can't go like this." He got up and looked in the mirror again. Definitely a hole in his beautiful black hair.

"Well, maybe she won't be there," I said.

"It's at her house!" he said.

That's right. Katie was on the Benefit committee with me. She'd come up with this idea to host a mini-party for all the pre-teens and early teens in the neighborhood. They could go off and have their own ball while we were having ours. Her nanny and maid were going to chaperone. Parents could pay for the privilege of having their children babysat during the Benefit and any proceeds would go to our charity. (That's right: I'm not telling you which charity. Then my efforts to disguise myself, this place, and all of these people would be for nothing. If I told you what the Benefit was for, you could find out who organizes it, and then you could find out who I am. Nope. Ain't gonna do that. I'm not on facebreak, twatter, googleminus, or whatever newfangled social media is out there for a reason.)

"Look, the party isn't for two days," I said. "Your hair might grow out a little by then. Saturday morning we could take you to get your hair cut, before the party."

"I don't have an appointment with Henri for three weeks," David said. "I'll never be able to get in on Saturday."

"We'll go somewhere else."

David gasped. I rolled my eyes. How could a 12-year-old boy give a shit where he got his hair cut?

I sighed. "Can we figure this out later? I've got to go into the city."

"You always want to figure things out later," he said. "But we never do."

He sounded suspiciously like his sister.

He better not decide to go through his teen years being a jerk. I wasn't going to put up with it again. I'd send him to military school. I would.

I put my arm across his shoulders and hugged him. Then I kissed the top of his head.

"I think you're really cute," I said.

"You always think I'm cute," he said. He sounded a bit mollified.

"Yep, and I'm always right."

"No, you're not."

"Yes, I am."

"No, you're not."

I laughed. "Yes, I am!"

He giggled. I began to tickle him. "Yes, I am! At least about this I am."

I kissed him again. "Spy on this Eartha woman while we're gone. See if she's up to no good. Then report back to me."

"You're leaving me with someone you think is up to no good?"

I got up and went to the door. "No, no, she's perfectly fine," I said. "As far as I know, all of the other families she stayed with survived. At least all the ones they can find."

"Funny, Mom," he said.

"Anything else going on at school I need to know about?" I asked.

He looked at me. He suddenly reminded me of his father. Hayword had been shy and awkward at this age, like David was now. But he got over it.

"Why are you asking?"

"Can't a mother be interested in her son's school life?" I asked.

"A mother can be, but you're not," he said.

He said it without malice, but I flinched anyway.

We paid his school a great deal of money. I figured they knew what they were doing, so I didn't have to know every little detail.

"I thought you liked it there," I said.

"I did," he said. He picked up his phone and looked at it. "I do. But it's been different lately. A lot of kids have had to drop out because they can't afford it. And we keep having those end of the world drills. I don't like them." He was silent as he looked at his phone.

I sat next to him again. I gently took away the phone.

"What end of the world drills?" I asked.

"You know, earthquake, fire, tsunami, terrorist attack, epidemics. I feel like I'm learning more about how it will all end than anything else. Did you know the ocean is getting higher every day? Every day. Our village could be underwater soon. Or at least the beachfront property."

"I don't know why they're doing tsunami drills," I said. "You're too high up. We're too high up. And we're not near the beach so we'll be okay. And the rest of the stuff is just living in California."

"Some of the kids are acting weird, too," he said.

"Are they bullying you?" I asked. "Hurting you? Because I'll go kick their asses. Or you and me together, we'll kick their asses. You know we could do it."

"Mom."

He was trying to tell me something. I knew it. I wasn't quite sure what to say.

"Okay," I said. "Is there something I can do? Do you want to go to another school?"

He shook his head and tried to get the phone from me.

"No," he said. "I dunno. Seems like everything is getting bad."

"I understand it must seem scary," I said. I was going to have to call the school and find out why they were scaring the shit out of my kid. "But look at us. We're doing all right. No floods, famine, fires."

"I heard some of the fathers have killed themselves," he said. "And some people are homeless now."

I shook my head. "Every time there's an economic shake-up, you always hear stories about people jumping out of buildings. But in real life, that doesn't happen. Or it rarely happens."

"I see every day in the news where some father has gone out and killed his wife and kids because he lost his job," David said, "or he came back from the wars and he lost his job and he goes out and kills people."

Man.

"You need to stop reading the news," I said.

"But I need to stay informed," he said.

"You're twelve years old!" I said. "You don't need to stay informed about any supposed apocalypse or any psycho fathers. Or whatever. All of that stuff is designed to scare the shit out of you. It's designed so that you keep coming back to that website again and again to find out the progress of whatever horror is going on—or supposedly going on. You need to promise me you'll stop looking."

"But you and Dad don't pay attention," he said. "Someone has to protect us."

"I protect us," I said. "And Daddy protects us. We pay enough attention. I may act like I don't pay attention, but I do."

That was a lie. I didn't read the paper or check anything newsworthy online. It was all horseshit. Maybe not all of it, but it was too difficult to wade through it all to find the truth.

Cuz the truth ain't out there?

"Your father and I won't let anything bad happen to our family."

"Something bad already happened," he said. "And it could happen again."

I had no answer for that.

"And you and Dad are hardly ever together," he said. "Are you getting a divorce?"

"No," I said. "Come on. Actually I'm going to see your father right now. We have a meeting together with a studio head."

My lover was driving me to the meeting, but my kid didn't need to know that.

"Really?" He perked right up. Geez Louise.

"And I'm late," I said. "So I better get going."

"Can I come?" he asked.

I chewed my lip. I should let him come. Blow off Mark and drive the two of us to L.A.

I should. I should spend quality time with my son.

Quality time trying to navigate L.A. traffic.

"Mom, your lip is bleeding," he said.

"What?" I put my finger on my lip. Looked at my finger: Blood. Apparently I had chewed my lip a little too hard.

"How about this?" I said. "You stay here and spy for me. Then your dad and I will come and have dinner with you. Just the three of us."

I held out his phone.

Relieved, he took it from me.

"Sure, Mom." But he was no longer paying any attention to me.

I hurried out of the room and down the stairs.

"See you later, Eartha!" I called.

"Have fun," she said.

I ran out the front door. I didn't see Mark's truck. I hurried down the drive and went out onto the road. Mark's truck was down the street a bit. I hurried toward it. He pushed the passenger door open from inside. I got up into the truck and slammed the door shut. He started the engine, and we headed down the road.

We smiled nervously at one another.

"So this is what it is like to be in a truck," I said.

"So this is what it is like to be in a truck with you," he said.

I laughed.

"Have you really never been in a truck?" he asked.

"Sure," I said. "My dad had one all while I was growing up. And Hayword had one for a while."

I could see a silver Mercedes coming around the bend toward us.

"Is that Joan?" I asked. I ducked down so that my head was nearly in Mark's lap.

"No, it wasn't her," he said.

"Hm," I said. "While I'm down here, is there anything you'd like me to do?"

He laughed. "Get up! You wanna get us both killed?"

I put on my sunglasses. Then I looked around Mark's very clean truck. I opened the glove compartment. Ah. Just what I was looking for: a baseball cap. I took it out and looked at it.

"The Dodgers, Mark?" I said. "Really? Come on. That's a sucker's team."

I put the cap on. Now no one would know me.

"Put on your seat belt," he said.

"No," I said. "I don't wear a seat belt. Except when I'm in the car with my son, to set a good example."

"Put on the seat belt or else I'm going to have to take you back home," he said.

"Fascist," I said.

"Yep."

I put on the seat belt.

"So you don't like the Dodgers?"

"What kind of team is it?" I asked. "Are they from New York

or are they from Los Angeles? And they never win anything."

"I've been going to Dodger games since I was a kid," he said. "My dad went to Dodger games when he was a kid. You don't know what you're talking about."

I made a noise.

"So who do you root for then?"

"I don't root for any of them," I said. "Like Seinfeld said, you're really only rooting for laundry now. And they're all so rich. Who gives a fuck any more?"

"You're talking about being rich?" he said.

"I'm not rich like baseball players are rich," I said. "We're writers. Or Hayword is. We're the lowest on the totem pole almost. Haven't you heard: No one in Hollywood can do a thing without writers, but no one in Hollywood has any respect for writers. We're all underpaid."

"I've been in your house," he said.

"Yeah, well, maybe we're overpaid, too," I said. "The whole fucking town is overpaid. Except the 99 percent who aren't. Or whatever the percentage is. I'm not complaining." Although it sounded like I was. "We started out in plays. The written word is more sacrosanct in the theater. But we got an offer on a script and we figured we'd take the money and run, start our own theater company. But you know, I didn't really like theater people. So many of them are so dramatic. I mean, they're fucking plays. Made up shit. Not brain surgery. There were so many divas. So we decided we'd come here for a while, to change things. Things got changed all right. Us things."

We drove out of the canyon and past the village. It was peaceful sitting in the truck quietly, watching the scenery. I couldn't remember the last time I had been a passenger in a car—or truck. Hayword and I always took separate cars wherever we went, in case one of us wanted to leave before the other, or in case I had a date—or a sudden burst of inspiration which would send me to the art studio. At least that was what I told Hayword.

It was strange Hayword never questioned me about the studio or what I did there. In the beginning he had asked if he could see some of the paintings. But then he stopped asking.

Didn't know what that meant. Figured he was respecting my space, man.

I smiled. "My space, man." Could be a title for a movie.

Mark took Highway 1 to 10. I leaned back, ready for the traffic. Or not ready for it. I had my left hand down on the seat. Mark put his hand over mine and squeezed it. I left my hand there for a minute. Let him have his domestic moment. Then he brought my hand up to his mouth and kissed the back of it.

"There," he said. "Now you can have it back."

The traffic wasn't bad. Although I didn't actually care.

"I don't know why I'm so talky today," I said. "Must be because I haven't had a drink all day."

"I don't mind it," he said. "I could listen to you rant about rich baseball players all day long. So there's no team you like?"

"When I was a kid, I liked the Tigers," I said. "Of course, we lived an hour from Detroit. My dad would take me to games at Tiger Stadium. Now that was a stadium. Loved it. Most of the time we listened to games on the radio. I loved that, too. Had to use my imagination."

"Your dad still around?"

"Sure," I said. "He and my mom live in Michigan half the year and go down to Florida the other half. He's been to some games at the new stadium—although I guess it's not that new any more—and he likes it. My dad's always been okay with what the world calls progress."

"Not you?"

"I like progress as much as the next gal, unless the next gal is a Luddite."

We slowed almost to a stop.

"Looks like there's an accident up ahead," Mark said. "Where am I taking you anyway?"

"Oh, yeah," I said. "It's called Juliet's and it's on Wilshire. Some of the studio execs like to go there, they say, because no one else goes there, but now everyone goes there."

"Do you know how to go there?"

I laughed. "Haven't a clue. I usually use my GPS which usually gets me lost and I drive around until I can find whatever place I'm looking for. Not that I go there very often. I don't come into the city much."

"Me, neither," he said.

"Where do you live?" I asked.

"Don't you remember?" he said. "You're the one who called me."

"No, I have no idea," I said. "I asked people at a party who they recommended. Katie Williams suggested you. She gave me your phone number. I never asked: Did you fuck her, too?"

Mark put both hands on the steering wheel.

He looked pissed.

"How long have we been seeing each other?" he asked.

"I don't know, Mark. What is going on up there?"

Seemed like someone was out of their car way up the freeway. Or someone was running down the highway.

Some lunatic, no doubt. L.A. County was rife with them.

All six lanes were now stopped.

The highway was a parking lot.

"Paved paradise and put up a parking lot," I sang quietly.

"You called me last February," he said. "It's been almost a year. Except for that month you were on vacation last summer, we've seen each other every week for months. How many times have I told you that I've never done anything like this before? I wish you wouldn't treat me like some goddamn gigolo."

"I wasn't on vacation for a month," I said.

"What the fuck?" Mark said. I followed his gaze.

Someone was running down the freeway. A man dressed in a dirty suit and tie.

He was yelling.

He was suddenly at the truck, almost on top of it, pounding on the hood.

His eyes were red, his hair filthy gray. His cheeks streaked with dirt and tears.

"Help me!" he yelled. "It's here. It's here. The end is here!"

Then he jumped off of the truck and kept running.

Mark laughed. We heard honking all around us. I looked at the drivers and passengers in the cars near us. People were laughing and talking.

"What the fuck was that?" Mark asked.

"Must be publicity for a movie," I said. "I wonder if they're doing another remake of *Invasion of the Body Snatchers.*"

A few moments later, the traffic started up again.

"Only in Hollywood," I said.

"Here we go," he said. "I think I might know where this restaurant is."

"Just put it in the GPS," I said.

"I'll find it," he said. "It'll be more of an adventure this way."

"An adventure where we get lost," I said. "You don't know some of these neighborhoods. They're dangerous."

"I do know all of these neighborhoods," Mark said. "I was raised here. Trust me. I'll get you there in one piece."

I really wanted to put the address into his GPS. I wanted to make him do what I wanted him to do.

But I took a deep breath. New experiences. I was supposed to have new experiences. Was supposed to learn to go with the flow.

"What did you mean you weren't on vacation?" he said.

"What do you mean what did I mean?"

"What?" he said. He glanced at me. "You're trying to avoid the fucking question. You said it. Now what did you mean?"

"Oh crap," I said. "I wasn't on vacation in last summer. I was in rehab."

"What?"

"Mark, pay attention to the road."

"You're just telling me this now?" he said.

"I never intended to tell you at all," I said. "My family was worried. I had made some apparently incoherent phone calls. Hayword found a place and took me there. I denied I was an alcoholic. I'd been using some of Joan's sleeping pills. I didn't steal them. She gave them to me. It was around the anniversary of Alberto's death and I often have a hard time then. So I mixed the pills with the alcohol. I went into rehab to shut everyone up. I stopped drinking while I was there. Easy as pie. I left a little earlier than they thought I should, but I've been on my best behavior since."

Mark shook his head. "I can't believe this."

"It was court mandated," I said. "I ran into the ditch by my driveway. Since I didn't hurt anyone and there was no proof that I was drunk, I got to keep my license, but I had to go to detox and rehab for at least three weeks. That's what I did. I don't know why you're so upset. I'm not an alcoholic. I like how I feel when I drink."

Mark laughed.

"What?"

"I think that's what every alcoholic says about drinking," he said.

"Everyone who drinks drinks because they like how they feel when they drink!" I said. "And they can't all be alcoholics!"

I didn't want to have this conversation. I was having too many conversations today that I didn't want to have.

"You know I don't drink," he said.

"Yes, I know you don't drink anything when we're together."

"Didn't you wonder why?"

"No," I said.

"Your lack of curiosity about anything but yourself is astounding."

"Hey, let's not get insulting," I said. "I have a complete lack of curiosity about my own life, too."

"I'm a fucking alcoholic," he said. "That's why I don't drink."

"You never told me that," I said. "Every *fucking* alcoholic I've ever known always tells me they're an alcoholic or they're in the program or they're a friend of Billy Bob or something the minute I meet them. You've never said anything."

"How do you know every alcoholic you've known has told you?" he said. "Maybe just as many didn't say anything."

"Well, I can't argue with you if you're logical," I said. "Okay, so you're an alcoholic. Did you ever suspect I was an alcoholic? Alkies must have an alkie-dar. No, you never suspected. So I'm not an alcoholic."

Mark shook his head and chuckled. One thing about Mark was that he laughed a lot when he was around me. He didn't find me offensive or perplexing. He seemed to think I was funny.

"I don't have any goddamn alkie-dar," he said, trying not to laugh. "No, it didn't occur to me that you were an alcoholic. You were sometimes sad. Now I know why."

"You don't know nothing," I said. "Don't think you know me because you've fucked me, or because I spilled my guts to you today. You don't."

"And don't think you can get mean with me because you're scared," he said. "I'm not your fucking enemy."

"Well, then who is? I'd like to find out so I'd have someone to blame and then I could shoot them, kill them, sue them, do something to make myself feel better."

I had said all of that out loud.

"Man," I said, "fuck me and the horse I rode in on."

Mark reached into his shirt pocket, pulled out his phone, and tossed it to me. I caught it.

"Can you read the text?" he asked.

"You read it," I said.

"I'm driving!"

"You are the biggest pussy in the world," I said. I read the text out loud to him. "'Giovanni tried to fix the sink. Water everywhere. Come quick!' There's an exclamation after 'quick.'"

"We've got to make a detour," he said. "Won't take long."

Mark got off at the next exit.

"Where are you going?" I asked. "I can't go down here. There's gangs. We'll get lost like Kevin Kline did in *Grand Canyon* and we'll be killed."

"He wasn't killed," Mark said. He headed away from the freeway, the gas stations, and fast food places. "Danny Glover saved him and they became lifelong pals. That could happen to us. But I gotta tell you, for living here for twenty years you don't know anything. We're nowhere near South Central. These are the 'burbs, man. You might see something you consider in bad taste, but that's about it. I don't live far from here."

"Oh Christ," I said. "You're kidnapping me, aren't you? I knew I should have never gotten into this truck."

Mark laughed. "Just shut the fuck up."

We were driving through a neighborhood. Reminded me of Michigan, actually, some one story houses, a few two story. Looked working class and up, I supposed.

"You really should get out more," he said.

"Why?"

"It's called living, darlin'," he said.

He pulled the truck up into the driveway of a small yellow ranch house. He got out, then leaned into the window on the driver's side of the truck. "I'll be right back, but you're welcome to come in."

He got a tool box from the back of the truck, and then he went up the walk and inside the house.

I sat in the truck and looked around. Wondered if this was where Mark had grown up. If the house had been red instead of yellow, it could have been my parents' house. Only theirs was two story. Surrounded by oak trees and maples. A single oak tree shaded this house. Up and down the street, I could see cars parked in driveways. Many of the houses had basketball hoops on the garages. I looked at my phone. I still wasn't late for the meeting I didn't want to go to.

I closed my eyes.

I could practically hear the minutes of my life ticking away. Tick. Tock. Tick. Tock.

I vaguely wondered what would happen if I got out and walked away.

I opened the door and got out of the truck. I glanced down the street and then back at the house. I shrugged and walked to the front door. I knocked. No one answered. I could hear loud voices inside.

I opened the screen door.

"Hello?" I called.

Again no one answered. I stepped inside. The house smelled like freshly baked bread. I looked around. A living room. Knick-knacks here and there. A sofa, the TV on with no sound, a cat watching me from a chair next to a small table with a sewing machine on it.

"Hello!" I walked into the living room. I looked to my right and saw the kitchen. Inside several people were talking anima-tedly. A man dressed in a T-shirt and jeans was drenched in water. A woman about the man's age, with black hair, seemed to be trying to reassure him. An older woman was gesturing and looking down at the wet floor.

I couldn't see Mark, but I heard him saying, "Christ, Giovanni, you're a fucking lawyer. What were you doing here?"

"Hello," I said.

The three people stopped talking and looked at me.

"I'm sorry," I said. "I knocked, but no one answered. Mark said I could come in."

"Come in, come in," the older woman said, gesturing.

I crossed the living room and went into the kitchen.

Seemed like water was everywhere. On the ceiling. On the walls. On the floor.

"Oh dear," I said. Not my normal expression, but that's what came out.

Mark got up from the floor near the sink. "You're not a plumber," he said. "You're not an electrician. Stop trying to do this crap. You gotta always turn off the fucking water."

"Mark," the older woman said. She looked at me.

"Mom, this is my friend Brooke," he said. "Brooke, this is my mother, Margaret Pantano. This is my sister Jane and my brother-in-law Giovanni."

"I think we should all know how to do stuff around the house," Giovanni said. "I'm trying to learn to be more useful."

"Then ask me," Mark said. "I'll teach you."

"Do you want some tea?" Margaret asked me.

"No, thank you," I said.

"We've got to get downtown," Mark said. "I'm giving her a ride to a meeting. She had some car trouble."

"Can I help you clean up?" I asked. Again, I'm not sure why I asked. Seemed like the polite thing to do.

"No," Jane said. "This is our mess. Giovanni and I will clean it up. Come on, Gio. Nice to meet you."

"When the timer rings, take out the bread," Margaret said. She grabbed a paper bag off the kitchen table and handed it to me. "Just took it out of the oven."

"Thank you," I said. I looked inside. A loaf of bread. "Don't you want it?"

"What am I gonna do with that bread?" she said. "I've got a million loafs. You eat it, you and my son. You could use some meat on your bones."

She put her hand on my elbow and led me out of the kitchen.

"I'm happy to meet you, Brooke," Margaret said. "I'm glad to see Mark is meeting new people. He says he has a girlfriend, but he never brings her around. He never goes out on the weekends. I think she's married which would mean he was committing adultery which is a mortal sin."

We were standing in the living room. Mark came up behind us. His shirt was wet. He was wiping his hands on a towel.

"Mom," he said. "Don't bore Mrs. Lightman with my personal life."

"He wouldn't be committing adultery," I said, "because he isn't married. She would be committing adultery."

"I don't believe in any of that Catholic stuff any more anyway," she said, waving her hand. "I only care that my son is happy."

"Mom," Mark said.

"What?" she said. "You need to find a woman who will birth you more babies. Men. I don't know how they get along in the world when they can't make their own babies."

"Can't we have this conversation another time?" Mark said. "When it would be less embarrassing."

"No," she said. "I haven't seen you in a week and you live two blocks away. Since I can't talk to you, I'll talk to her. She looks like a good listener."

"Looks are deceiving," I said.

Margaret laughed. "She's a funny one. Don't you think he should have more babies?"

"I don't want any more children," Mark said. "Good grief. I've got to go." He kissed his mother on the cheek. Then he put his hand on my back to propel me out the door.

I gotta tell ya: I really wanted to find some back alley and have sex with him then and there.

We both left the house and hurried out to the truck.

"Thanks for saving us," his mother called as we left.

I got into the truck next to Mark. He started the truck and drove away. I waved to his mother.

When we were out of sight of the house, I started to laugh.

"It's not funny," he said. "I don't know what the fuck got into her."

"Aw, come on," I said. "It was sweet. The mother trying to get her son married with children. And the brother-in-law who can't do anything. It's very domestic. Better than TV."

"Hey, don't romanticize us," Mark said. "We're as dysfunctional as anyone."

"If you thought I was romanticizing what I just saw, then I said it wrong."

I reached into the paper bag and ripped off a couple pieces of bread. I gave Mark a piece and I ate the other one.

"Man, this is pretty damn good. If Eartha had made it, it would definitely be her one great thing today."

"What?" Mark asked.

"Long story," I said. "I'll tell you later."

Or I wouldn't.

"Giovanni has been out of work for a while," Mark said. "I think he's going stir crazy."

"Where are you taking us?" I asked. "Aren't we going back to the freeway?"

"No," he said. "Just sit back and relax."

"Do you know any place where we can stop and do it, quickly?" I asked. "Before my meeting."

"My house is a few blocks away," he said.

I thought about it. I did. But then that would seem too much like a date. And I would know where he lived. It was bad enough that I'd met his family.

"No," I said. "No. I better get to the meeting. So you've got another married woman you're seeing?"

He looked at me. I laughed.

"I'm so glad my parents pay little or no attention to my life," I said. "She knew I was your married lady. She's not stupid."

"No, she's not," he said. "But I don't think she knows."

"By the way, my name is not Mrs. Lightman," I said. "Don't call me that."

"But I've heard you on the phone," he said. "You always call yourself Brooke Lightman. When you first called me, you called yourself Brooke Lightman."

"Yeah, well, my name is Brooke McMurphy," I said. "That's how I signed the marriage license, so that's my legal name. I wrote under Brooke McMurphy. My friends called me Mac. I felt more like a Mac than a Brooke. But with the kids and everything, it just became easier to call myself Lightman. Everyone thought McMurphy was my husband's name anyway. But it sounded weird today, to hear you call me that."

"Okay," he said. "Duly noted. They called you Mac?" He glanced at me. "I don't see it. You're clearly a Brooke to me."

"A river maybe," I said. "A raging river. An ocean. But not a brook. That sounds like such a nothing and nobody name."

Mark shrugged. "I never thought about it before. When I hear the name now, I think of you. Strong, funny, beautiful, smart."

I moved across the seat until I was sitting next to him. He put his right arm around me and I put my head on his shoulder. We drove like that for a while. I felt strangely peaceful. He kissed the top of my head.

Then we were in traffic again and I moved away. Too many cars, too many people. Sometimes in these situations I felt a little overwhelmed. Completely overwhelmed, actually. This was when I really wanted a drink.

That did not make me an alcoholic. Come on. Modern society was fucking overstimulating. My nervous system had long ago fried itself out. Maybe everyone was completely burned out, too, and I couldn't tell. Sometimes it seemed as though everyone else was moving through life so easily. I tried to emulate those people who were doing it right.

Or seemed to be doing it right.

Maybe they were all pretending. Maybe we were all make-believe made-up people.

"That's it right up there," Mark said. "Do you want me to drop you off out front or a block away?"

I made a noise. "I don't want to go," I said.

But at least there I could get a drink.

"Then don't go," he said. "Come with me to the beach. Or back to my house. Or we could go to a movie. You love movies."

I looked at him. I couldn't remember the last time I had gone out to see a movie.

"What makes you think I love movies?"

"Because you're always quoting from movies," he said. "Or saying that this or that is like this or that movie."

"Really? I do that?"

"Sure," he said. "You talk about books, too. But more often it's movies."

"Huh," I said. I shook my head. I didn't have time to think about that or wonder why. I didn't love movies. I didn't like movies. They were so fucking fake. Everything turned out in movies even when it didn't, and if it didn't, I didn't want to see it. Or hear about it.

"Thanks, Mark," I said. "You can pull in here. I'll walk the rest of the way. I appreciate it. It's been an interesting day."

He pulled into a parking lot down the block from Juliet's. He parked the truck. I started to get out.

"Brooke," Mark said.

I turned around and looked at him.

"I'm going to see you again, aren't I?" He looked right into my eyes. He did that a lot. Wasn't sure I liked it.

"Um," I said.

He shook his head. "I knew it. You're thinking of ending this, aren't you? Because you told me all that stuff today. And now you know things about me. You've met my mother. You know I'm an alcoholic. Who hasn't had a drink in many years, by the way. So now it's time to say goodbye because if we didn't break up, then it would feel too much like a relationship."

I sighed. "Please don't try to psychoanalyze me."

"That's not what I'm doing," he said. "I'm speaking the truth, aren't I?"

"Yes," I said. "I guess. I've got to go. Yes, I would like to throw your ass to the curb now because you know a little tiny bit about me. Yes, I would like to throw your ass to the curb because I had no idea we had been doing this for a fucking year! Almost. But I happen to enjoy your ass and I'm not ready to make that decision or any decision right now. I've got to go to this fucking meeting."

"I've got another job up in the canyon Monday," he said. "How about I meet you at your place around lunch time."

"If I agree, will you stop talking and let me leave?"

"Hey, you've been free to go at any time," he said. "You'll always be free to go at any time. I've known and understood the rules."

I took off the baseball cap and ran my fingers through my hair.

"Your mom saw me in this dirty old baseball cap," I said. "What must she think?"

I kissed Mark on the mouth, then handed him the baseball cap.

"Later, gator."

FIVE

It was noisy outside Juliet's—and much too sunny. I stepped eagerly into the dimly lit restaurant. I looked around. The restaurant was noisy, too, and nearly full. On the other side of the room was the patio, surrounded by ferns and trees. I bet it was quieter out there.

Where was Hayword?

I had forgotten to call him and tell him I was twenty minutes out. Maybe they weren't here yet.

Then I saw Hayword stand up. He was outside on the patio. His long lanky figure seemed to unfold itself from his chair. He smiled when he saw me, like David had earlier, and he waved. I waved back and hurried across the restaurant floor and out onto the patio.

Hayword walked toward me and took my hand. He squeezed it. His way of reassuring me, I supposed. He held out a chair for me and I turned and saw the other two people at the table.

"Sally St. James!" I said.

"Brooke McMurphy," the woman said.

We leaned toward one another and kissed the air next to our cheeks. I sat down as Hayword pushed my chair in for me.

"Wow," I said. "Long time. Hayword didn't tell me."

"I had forgotten you two knew one another," he said. "And this is Irving Jackson. Irving is one of the creative execs and Sally is now studio head."

I shook Mr. Jackson's hand. He was probably in his forties, with dyed black hair, maybe a weave, dressed in khakis and a knit shirt with a jacket on over it all. He was trying to dress casually, but he was not casual or comfortable.

Sally looked like she always had looked: gorgeous. Her black hair was shoulder-length now, flipped up like Marlo Thomas used to wear on *That Girl* a long time ago. Decades ago. What had made me think of that? She wore a sleeveless red dress. She was slender and tanned. I remembered she hadn't a tan line on her whole body.

"Don't pay any attention to our titles," Sally said. "We're redesigning everything. Or re-inventing everything. What Irving is good at is getting things going. I saw the script for *Zombie Town,* and I was blown away. I think this can be a blockbuster. Jack Meredith is ready to go. But both of us want some changes. We know the kids will go see it. And that's good. But we're not sure the girls will go back to see it again. I like the idea of making this a zombie movie girls will flock to. And a zombie movie sophisticated enough for adults."

I looked at Hayword, and he smiled. He looked downright giddy.

"We've got the makeup figured out," Irving said. "And we're pretty much all set with the special effects. We want to shoot this picture quickly and get it in the theaters quickly. Make it seem like a home movie movie. You know what I mean. That's Meredith's idea. And he's a genius at this kind of thing. We've scouted locations in your area, actually. We can be ready to shoot before the month is out."

"What?" I said. "How's that possible if you don't have a completed script?"

The three of them laughed.

Sally said, "Brooke, you've been in this business a long time. You know we can do it. Hayword wrote a brilliant script. Having the zombies really be aliens from another planet: That was brilliant. But we need understory. We need some of your humor and brilliant dialogue."

This was one of the things I hated about Hollywood meetings. Everything was brilliant, perfect, awesome, a real moneymaker.

Come on. A zombie movie could not be brilliant.

"I don't write much any more," I said.

"Bullshit," Sally said. "Everyone in Hollywood knows you doctor Hayword's scripts."

I looked at Hayword. He didn't say anything.

"That's not true," I said. "I check his spelling."

"The fucking computer can do that," Sally said. "You two together are brilliant."

I leaned my head back. I had planned on being as hospitable as possible. But all of this *brilliance* was getting on my nerves.

"Would you care for anything?" the waiter stopped and asked me.

"A gin and tonic," I said, "with more gin than tonic. And some bread."

"Even if I was doing any doctoring," I said, "I'm not interested in a zombie movie. I wouldn't know what to write."

"We want it a little more sexy," Sally said.

"A little more sexy?" I asked. "You mean it's sexy now?"

Sally laughed. She looked at me and smiled. I wondered if she was remembering us naked together, too.

"Actually it's not sexy at all," Sally said. "We want you to make zombies sexy the way vampires are sexy now. Or were-wolves."

"Well, Sally, as I told Hayword when he mentioned this all to me, zombies aren't sexy. Who would want to have sex with a zombie?"

"Anyone who is married to a banker is already having sex with a zombie whether they like it or not," Sally said.

Irving half-smiled. Hayword looked worried.

The waiter brought my gin and tonic.

I sucked it down dry.

I glanced at Hayword. He was drinking a beer.

I ordered another gin and tonic.

Someone brought me bread and butter.

Nothing better with gin and tonic than bread and butter.

I slathered the butter on the bread and took a bite.

Wasn't as good as Margaret's. Damn. I'd left the loaf in Mark's truck.

When the waiter put the second gin and tonic on the table, I said, "I don't think it's sexy when flesh is falling off of some-one. It's disgusting. It's not sexy when the dead are eating one another."

"Have you read the script?" Sally asked.

I shook my head.

"She hasn't had a chance," Hayword said.

Sally looked at Irving.

He cleared his throat. "I'm going out for a smoke," he said. "You wanna come?" He said that last bit to Hayword.

"You don't mind?" Hayword asked.

I shook my head. The men excused themselves, then walked away.

Once they were gone, Sally leaned back in her chair.

"Hiya, Mac," she said. "I've missed you. Long time."

I nodded. "What's going on with this picture, anyway? Why the rush?"

"I'm trying to make my name," she said. "We need an influx of easy money. I think this will do it—if we're all still around by the time it comes out. Seems like everything is going to hell in a hand basket. Zombies are big now. Everything's a 'zombie.' They call those half-finished subdivisions 'zombie developments.' The kids talk about us all being corporate zombies, shilling for the man. There's some skin condition going around that some people are calling the zombie plague. Zombies, zombies, zombies. But the movies about them suck, so to speak. They're B movies, if that. They gross people out. Who wants to eat popcorn while watching people getting eaten? We want this movie to do for zombie movies what *Forbidden Planet* did for science fiction movies. MGM went all out on that movie. They took it very seriously. They wanted it to be a blockbuster."

"But it wasn't," I said. "It didn't do well."

"This one will be a blockbuster," she said. "It will do well."

"So you want it to be the same as *Forbidden Planet* but different," I said.

"See, you do understand Hollywood."

"I don't know what you think I can do to help," I said.

"Just read the script," she said. "See if you can humanize it. We'll pay you lots of money. Additional money. Don't forget to leave an opening for a sequel."

"A sequel? I don't want to think about a sequel."

"You should," Sally said. "Remember *Thelma and Louise.* They could have made a mint with *Thelma and Louise.* It could have been a very successful movie."

"They did make a mint," I said, "and it was a very successful movie."

"But think what could have been," she said, "if the final shot was of a hand coming up over the ledge. Sequels galore!"

I laughed. "I suppose you're envisioning Thelma and Louise dolls. T-shirt. Mugs. The whole shebang."

Sally St. James smiled. "Never underestimate the power of an iconic image."

"Them flying over the Grand Canyon was iconic enough for me."

"I'm just saying," Sally said. "Will you at least look at Hayword's script?"

"All right," I said. "I'll read it. I'm not sure when I'll get to it. I've got this benefit on Saturday. After that, though."

"Any chance you could read it sooner?" she said. "Like maybe take it down to your love nest and read it there. Shouldn't take more than a couple of hours. I could even meet you there and read it with you." She smiled. "You know I fuck all of my writers, so it's gonna either be you or Hayword, and I seem to remember you said you'd kill him if he ever cheated on you again. So—" She shrugged. "—you'd be saving his life."

I smiled. "You're so full of shit, Sally."

She laughed. "Yeah, you could always see through me."

"I can see your wedding ring," I said. "You always said if you got married you'd never fool around."

"I know," she said. "What an idiot I was. But I've been true to my word. I don't cheat on him. I don't fool around any more. Not since you broke my heart."

"You never had a heart," I said. "That's why we worked well together."

"And played well together."

We were silent for a few moments.

"How are you really?" she asked.

Like I was going to tell her.

Like I knew.

"I'm fine," I said. "When did you get married?"

"Don't you read the papers?" she asked. "Six years ago.

We've got a son and a daughter. I married someone who is not in the business, thank God. He's a normal guy with a normal life."

"Really?" A plumber? Electrician? Teacher? "What's he do?"

"He's the CEO at one of the biggest investment firms here in L.A.," she said.

I laughed. "That's a normal guy with a normal life?"

"Yes," she said. "I didn't say he was poor. He's normal because he's not in the business."

"He's not in trouble with all this economic stuff going on?" I asked.

She shrugged. "He says he's not. We seem to be doing okay. Plus I make a great deal of money." She smiled. "And I can make you a great deal money, too. I think writers are treated like shit and I'd like to help you out. Just like I did way back then. It was my idea to give you points on *Love and Other Insanities.* Did I ever tell you that?"

"Yes, every time we fucked each other you reminded me."

She grinned. "I wanted you to appreciate me. Gawd." She looked around. "I really need a smoke."

"I don't remember you smoking," I said.

"Why do you think I went out on the back porch all the time?" she asked.

I shrugged. "I don't know. I'm not very attentive. Go out with Irving and have a smoke."

"I can't," she said. She looked around again. "I quit smoking. And I signed a contract, a pre-nup, that if Jonathan ever found out I was smoking again, that would be grounds for divorce."

"Does he want a divorce?" I asked.

"I don't think so," she said, "but lately I've felt like someone is following me. And that made me nervous so I started smoking again."

I laughed.

"It's not funny," she said.

"I know," I said. "It's ridiculous. Why don't you just quit smoking?"

"I don't like anyone telling me what to do," she said.

I understood that.

"So you'll kill yourself to spite him?" I asked.

Like I should fucking talk.

"Come out with me," she said. "You can hold the cigarette and pretend it's yours and I'll smoke it."

"I'd rather go make out," I said. Although I didn't really. She had been a pain in the ass. One thing about having men as lovers, generally speaking, they didn't have troubling getting off. Sally had to have it in the right place at the right time.

And as I said, I was not really that attentive.

"Making out with someone is probably grounds for divorce, too," she said. "And I'm never getting divorced. They'll have to pry my cold dead fingers off his balls before I get a divorce."

"That's a pretty picture," I said. I motioned to the waiter. "We'll be right back."

Sally got her purse, and she and I walked through the now nearly deserted restaurant and out the door. The street was lined with customers having a smoke, including Irving. Hayword stood next to Irving, his hands in his pockets.

We went back inside. I followed Sally through the kitchen and out back. No one tried to stop us. No one said a word. We went by the overturned milk cartons where two of the kitchen workers sat having a smoke. Sally walked to the alley and leaned against the wooden fence.

She looked around. "Seeing if they've got cameras," she said. Then she took out a cigarette and lit it. She handed it to me.

I put it between my forefinger and middle finger. I had never smoked. I didn't know what to do with it.

"Hold it like you enjoy it," she said. "Hold it like you'd like to fuck it."

"Sally, that's disgusting," I said. "And this is ridiculous."

She leaned over and took a drag. She held the smoke in her lungs for a moment. Then she turned to the fence and let the smoke out through the slats.

"Much better," she said. "Much better." She sighed. "So how's the love nest these days?"

"I'd rather not talk about it," I said.

"The kids okay?" she asked.

She was acting as if we were old friends. Intimate friends. We had been intimate, but we were never friends. At least I didn't think so. Just like Mark and I were not friends. No one I had ever brought to the art studio was a personal friend of mine.

"The kids are fine," I said. "Everyone is fine."

"Speaking of fine," Sally said. She looked over by the kitchen door. Mark was standing there with a waiter next to him who was pointing to us.

"I bet he works out," she said.

I started to say, "He doesn't work out; he works for living." But I had been living this double life for so long that I was used to keeping my mouth shut until I knew the lay of the land.

Mark stepped down out of the restaurant and walked toward us.

What was he doing here?

Before I could say or do anything, he held out my pocketbook and the bag of bread Margaret had given me.

"You left these in the cab," he said.

He wasn't lying. I had left them in the cab of the truck.

"I thought you might need them," he said.

I took the bread and pocketbook from him.

"Thank you," I said.

Mark glanced at the cigarette in my hand. Then he nodded to

both of us. He turned around and walked down the alley toward the street.

"He was your cab driver?" Sally asked. "I would have done him in a second." She took another drag on the cigarette.

Then I dropped the cigarette on the ground and rubbed it out with my foot. I picked it up and threw it in the trash.

"It's been a long day," I said, "and I've got a script to read."

We went back into the restaurant. Irving and Hayword were waiting for us at the table. We all talked for a bit, and then Hayword and I said our goodbyes and left. Hayword was more than a little surprised that I was going home with him.

We got into the car together.

"I feel like we're on a date," Hayword said as he pulled out of the parking lot and onto the street. "It's been so long since we've been in the car together."

The day was starting to wear on me and I was less and less talky. Maybe if we had stopped by a bar on the way home, but David was waiting for us at home. We'd be in traffic for a while.

"Was it nice to see Sally again?" Hayword asked. He was trying to make small talk. We'd known each other over thirty years and he was trying to make small talk with me.

"She's looking good," I said. "She's got two kids now. And a husband who will divorce her if he catches her smoking."

"Really?" He glanced over at me.

"Yep," I said. "It's in her pre-nup."

"What was in our pre-nup?" he asked.

I didn't say anything. He was trying to joke with me.

I wasn't in the mood.

Why was it always easier to be nicer to strangers or people who were not family?

"How'd you get to L.A. today?" he asked.

When telling a lie, it was always better to tell as much truth as possible. Meant I didn't have to remember as much.

"Joanie had some trouble at her house today," I said. I wouldn't tell him the gory details. No need. "I went over to help her out. The plumber was there, you know, the guy we used."

"Mark Pantano," he said. "I remember him. Seemed like a nice guy."

I glanced at him. Why would he remember Mark Pantano, our plumber?

"I mentioned I was going into Los Angeles and he was on his way there, so he offered to give me a lift."

"I'm surprised you said yes," Hayword said.

He drove us out onto the freeway. Everyone was driving too fast, and it was too crowded.

"I wish you'd put on your seat belt," he said.

I didn't argue with him. I put on the belt.

"I'm glad you got a ride," he said. "It's good for you to get out and see people."

"Don't talk about me like I'm sick," I said. "I'm not sick."

"Wasn't saying you were," he said.

"I don't know how you do this drive almost every day," I said. "I would go crazy."

"Gets me away from the house," he said.

He said it too quickly. I could tell he was sorry he had said the truth.

"If this trip is hard on you," I said, "you should start using your office in the house again. We won't bother you. It'll be nice and quiet."

I had my left hand on my leg. Hayword put his hand over my hand and squeezed it.

"Won't it be nice to work together again?" he said. "I always loved our collaborations. You the brains, me the brawn. You the lover, me the—" He stopped. "What does follow that?"

"I don't know," I said.

He took my hand and started to raise it to his lips.

No.

That was too weird.

I pulled my hand away.

"David had a tough time at school," I said. "Had gum in his hair all day and no one told him. Then I told him about it and he went a little hysterical, you know the way he gets. So I cut it out for him and that made it worse. Well, maybe not worse but not better. Don't know what we're going to do about it. And he said they've been doing all these drills in school to teach them about emergencies. It's scaring him a little. I told him he had to stop watching the news for a while. So if you see him watching, please encourage him not to."

"Maybe we could tell him the news is really like a movie," he said. "It's all make-believe."

"I wonder how far from the truth that actually is," I said.

"I can't wait for you to read the script," he said.

I shrugged. "I was going to fuck you tonight. But if you'd rather I read the script, I will."

"Can't you do both?" he asked.

"At the same time? Sure. Why not? But in the future I may associate having sex with you with zombies. Your call."

I was ready to be home when we finally got there. I wanted a bath, a shower, or a highball. Maybe all three.

But I had promised dinner with my kid, and I was not going to break that particular promise.

When Hayword and I walked through the door together—that hadn't happened in a while—David came running out of the kitchen toward us.

His hair was short. And spiky. No more hole in his head.

He looked good. And he was smiling.

"Wow, kiddo!" I said. "Turn around. You are the dude!"

"Hey, buddy," Hayword said. "Lookin' good."

"It's Eartha," David said excitedly. "Eartha did it." We all walked into the kitchen where Eartha sat at the table. She smiled.

"You can do hair?" I asked.

"Sure," she said. "We looked online for some styles he liked and then we did it. I told him he was taking a chance letting me cut his hair, but he was willing to take that chance."

David beamed.

"And we made dinner," David said. "I helped. It was so much fun. We're ready to eat. Can Eartha eat with us?"

I laughed. "Sure," I said.

"Go wash your hands, David," Eartha said.

He ran from the room.

I looked at her. "So this isn't *Hand That Rocked the Cradle* or anything, is it? Cuz I don't have asthma. I'll whip your butt if you try to steal my kids or my husband."

Hayword laughed. "I'm gonna wash up, too."

"No," Eartha said. "If you'll remember, the Rebecca De Mornay character didn't fare well in that movie. And I've never lost a child."

Oh man. I had forgotten that part of the movie.

Who cared? It was a stupid demented movie anyway.

"In any case," I said, "thank you for that. He looks great. More importantly, he's happy. I'd say that's your one great thing today."

"And you haven't even eaten dinner yet," she said.

We had a nice dinner, the four of us. I can't remember what we talked about. Maybe we listened to David talk about his day. Afterward, David went to his room, Eartha went to the garden house, and Hayword and I went to our room. He gave me a printed copy of *Zombie Town.*

"First thing we've got to do is change the title," I said.

We got naked together. He tried to go down on me, but I

wouldn't let him. Seemed too personal. But he did his best to rock my world. And he succeeded. Then he wanted to cuddle. I was so tired I actually did it. I put my head on his shoulder and let him hold me.

"Remember when we were kids planning our lives together?" he whispered.

I nodded.

"Did you ever imagine we'd be where we are?" he said. "We are so fortunate."

I didn't say anything. I wanted to scream. I wanted to cry. I wanted to feel something besides this vast emptiness that seemed to grower wider by the day.

I wanted to hit Hayword. Instead, I turned away and pretended to sleep.

When I heard Hayword sleep breathing, I got out of bed, got my phone, and went into the bathroom. I texted Mark, "It wasn't my cigarette."

Why on Earth had I texted that? I wanted to take it back, but I got an immediate answer. "Really? Phew, I thought maybe my smoke-dar was off. Thinking of you. Love."

I shook my head, turned off the phone, and went back to bed.

SIX

I heard Hayword and David laughing when I woke up. I lay under the sheet listening. Sounded like they were in David's room. Must be about time to leave for school. Or maybe time to go down for breakfast.

I turned my head and looked at the clock.

Why was I awake so early?

Didn't even have a hangover.

What were they saying to one another? How easy they seemed together. Like friends, buddies. Or father and son.

Would Alberto and Hayword have been buddies? Would he have been like me? Or like David? Like Fern? Hopefully not like Fern. I didn't hate my daughter, no matter what it sounds like. I didn't. I didn't like her. It was hard to like someone who had been so consistently unkind for so many years.

Perhaps that was the way Hayword felt about me. Did he think I was consistently unkind to him? Or maybe inconsistently unkind.

Who cared?

The laughter had stopped. I could hear them going downstairs. I thought about going down and joining them for breakfast. We could have another family meal. Like normal people.

Did normal people eat together? When I was a kid, we had eaten together as a family. Sometimes it had been torture. My little brother didn't like to eat anything. My sister ate everything. And I was always mouthing off to my parents. At least in my teen years. So, often, dinner consisted of me saying something and then my father slapping me across the face.

Words. Smack. Words. Smack.

I must have been a terror when I was a teen.

Maybe Fern had gotten it from me.

Only I had grown out of it. Fern hadn't.

My father didn't remember hitting me. Swore he didn't do it, would never have hit his own dear child.

Once he got mad at me and took a hold of my arms and shook me, hard. The house was full of relatives. I was wearing jeans and a pajama top and the top came unbuttoned as he shook me. I wasn't wearing anything underneath the top. My father kept shaking me, and there I was with my beautiful teen breasts exposed to everyone.

It was a deeply humiliating experience.

Not that it scarred me for life. I didn't believe in that psychological bullshit.

What was past was past.

"Goddamn it, goddamn it," I said.

I did not want to think about any of this.

Today I was having lunch with some of the other Enclave women who were organizing the Benefit. We were meeting at a restaurant in the hotel where the Benefit would be. (Let's call it the Shilton Hotel and leave it at that.) I didn't know why I was going to the lunch or to the Benefit. I hadn't done much this year.

We'd donated some money; I'd called some donors. I'd gotten the hotel to give us a deal. Beyond that, I was along for the ride. I guess I was going because I had been taking part in the Benefit for years, even before.

Before Alberto died.

I wondered if my life would always be before and after?

Or would it change when someone else in my life died? If I died, would my children talk about their lives as before and after Mom died?

I got out of bed and took a quick shower. Then I got dressed and went downstairs. Hayword and David sat at the kitchen table eating. Eartha was at the stove. She looked up and smiled at me. How domestic she looked standing there in her apron.

"I thought I heard you moving around up there," she said. "I found this bag of stale bread and wondered if you would like some French toast made from it, with strawberries and powdered sugar on top?"

"Shouldn't my son have something more substantial for breakfast?" I asked.

"I fed him oatmeal with fresh fruit and a scrambled egg," she said.

"It was good, Mom," David said. "Better than cereal."

"You like oatmeal?" I asked. I couldn't imagine anyone liking oatmeal.

"Sure," David said. He seemed so animated. And his hair still looked good.

"Yep, I liked it, too," Hayword said. "It'll stick to my ribs."

"The French toast was for you," Eartha said. "I didn't want your homemade bread to go to waste."

French toast for breakfast. Wasn't that kind of like having dessert for breakfast? I could definitely go for that.

"Hey, if you wanna make it," I said, "then I wanna eat it."

I went over to the kitchen table. Hayword put his arm around my waist and drew me near as I stood between him and David. I put my arm across his shoulders.

"We need groceries," Hayword said. "You care if Eartha uses your car?"

"You can drive?" I asked Eartha. "I thought you were a little hippie girl who was against the combustion engine and everything."

Eartha laughed. She was slicing Margaret's bread. "I'm too young to be a hippy," she said. "I do believe we have to get off oil, but I blame big business more than I blame the average person. Most people do what's easiest and what everyone else is doing—which is just walking around pretty senseless, following the crowd."

Wasn't sure what that had to do with anything.

"Like the zombies in your movie," David said. He put his arms out straight in front of him and rocked back and forth. "Take me to your oil or I'll eat you."

Hayword laughed. "It's *our* movie," he said. "Your mom is working on it, too."

I groaned. Did he really have to tell anyone I was working on a zombie movie?

"Cool," David said.

"Whether we are zombies or not begs the questions," I said. "Eartha, can you drive?"

"Sure," Eartha said. "Unless you want to take me. We could go grocery shopping together. That would be fun."

I looked at her. Who was this woman? I thought she'd be a huge disruption in our house—I mean, she wore Rasta braids for chrissakes. Yet now she seemed almost like a cipher. She went along, got along, did whatever we needed her to do.

She hadn't done something to Violeta's mother in order to weasel her way into our family, had she?

I wasn't sure what movie that had come from.

But it seemed plausible.

I stared at her.

Actually, it didn't seem plausible. She didn't seem particularly nefarious.

Those were the people to watch out for: the non-nefarious ones.

Oh lord. I was tiring myself out, and it wasn't even eight a.m. yet.

"I won't be going grocery shopping," I said. Unless hell froze over. "I've got a meeting in the city today. We're tying down the details for the Benefit. Or nailing them down. Whatever someone does with details."

I sat next to David while he finished eating. Hayword looked at me and winked. The morning after we had sex, he was always happy, hopeful. I was certain he was certain that now everything would go back to the way it had been before.

"I put the script in your office," he said.

My office?

Oh yes. That room I never went into. Next to his office.

I nodded. "Thank you."

He was waiting for more.

"What are you doing today?" I asked.

"The director wants more changes on *Powerbreakers,*" he said. "I don't know if I can change one more word."

Hayword always said that, but he kept rewriting, any time anyone asked. He was easygoing, easy to work with, a pleasant guy who would do anything to make everyone else's lives easier, even if it pained him.

I had read the *Powerbreakers* script. It was about lawyers working in a big corporation who discover their bosses are working with politicians to assassinate the president and take over the government. He originally had three main characters, three lawyers, all young dewy-eyed men. Nobody takes them seriously or listens to their findings. One of them gets killed pretty early on and then the other two have to run for their lives and expose the conspiracy.

After I read it, I suggested this to Hayword, "Make the two surviving lawyers women. And make the woman at the farmhouse—the one who cooks for the men and sleeps with one of them—change her to a man. Don't change any of the dialogue of the characters."

"None of it?" he said.

"Nope," I said. "Remember that's what Alan Ladd, Jr. did when he got the script for *Alien*. He said make the main character a woman, put another woman in it, and don't change the dialogue. See how that turned out."

I had heard that story for decades and didn't knew if it was apocryphal or not, but I told it to Hayword then. He rewrote the script as I suggested and the studio loved it, thought it was perfect, great, brilliant. When could he start the rewrite?

The studio kept trying to tart up the women. Hayword fought them on that. Fortunately the director was on his side.

I kept telling him I was tired of hearing about it. He should tell them he was finished with it. Let someone else do it if they wanted any more rewrites. But I was glad he had stuck with it. Some other asshole would have come in and rewritten it so that one of the women got raped or tortured or at least fucked in the ass. Those were often the kind of changes the studio wanted.

"I'm proud of you for sticking with it," I said.

He looked at me, surprised.

"Really?"

"Sure," I said. "It would have been a lot easier to give in to them, to let it go."

"I keep thinking of Fern," he said. "These women aren't much older than Fern. I want to keep them safe, safe even in an unreal world."

"I forgot to tell you," David said. "Fern texted me she was coming to Los Angeles this weekend."

"Really?" I said. "To see us?"

"I don't know," David said.

I did not want to deal with my daughter right then.

Eartha brought over a pile of French toast and set it next to me, along with maple syrup.

"Have you eaten?" I asked Eartha.

"Yep," she said. "Bright and early after my yoga. I'll clean up and go shopping, if that's okay."

"Sure, there's an extra house key and car key over by the house phone," I said, pointing. Yesterday I couldn't and wouldn't leave her in the house alone. Now I was giving her the keys to my house and my very expensive car.

"And I'll make certain I'm home by the time David gets out of school," Eartha said. "Mr. Lightman said Mrs. Williams was driving him home."

I glanced at David. He grinned at me. He was going to get to ride home with his girlfriend.

"Okay," I said. "But you don't have to call him Mr. Lightman. His name is Hayword. I'm Brooke. You don't work for us."

Eartha smiled, but she didn't say anything.

I put several pieces of French toast on my plate. I scooped up some strawberries from a bowl already on the table. Then I poured maple syrup over all of it. If only I had a screwdriver to drink with it: orange juice and vodka. Oh man. Perfect.

I cut into the toast, stabbed if with a fork, then brought it up and into my mouth.

I chewed.

Oh. My. God.

How did she do it?

"I want to have sex with this French toast," I said.

David giggled.

"I think I need a bite of that," Hayword said. He picked off a piece of it from my plate with his fork and ate it. "That is good."

David picked up his fork.

"No," I said, "you're too young for this."

He laughed and quickly speared a piece of toast and put it on his plate. Then he ate some.

"Such a child," I said.

"I don't know if I want to have sex with it," David said, "but I might want to dance with it."

"I don't want to hear this kind of talk from my son," I said.

I kept eating.

"I'm glad you like it," Eartha said.

"Is this your one great thing?" I asked. "Because it is pretty damn good."

"We'll see," she said.

I was soon alone in the house.

I did not want to go to Los Angeles again today. Maybe I could get out of it.

I called Joan. "I don't want to go to the city," I said. "We all live here. Let's have the meeting here. We can meet outside by my pool."

"Come on," Joan said. "Katie is having her chauffeur drive us. We can drink all the way in. And gossip."

"I don't gossip," I said.

"But you do drink," Joan said. "And Melissa Peake is coming."

"She never has anything nice to say about anyone," I said.

"I know!" Joan said. "That's why it'll be so much fun."

"I don't like any of you," I said.

"And we don't like you," Joan said. "Another reason it'll

be so much fun. Come on. You can tell them about rescuing me from the tub."

"You made me swear never to tell anyone," I said. "I keep my promises."

Well, I kept those kinds of promises.

"Okay," Joan said. "Please come for me. Those women scare me. You never let them get away with anything."

"All right," I said. "But I'm wearing something slutty. And if I see anyone fuckable, I'm gonna fuck them."

"I love it when you talk dirty," she said.

I went upstairs and found something to wear. Something a little bit see-through. Low cut. I liked dressing like a cougar. I liked trying to look ridiculous and then taking it back, a little, so no one could be sure if I was completely tasteless or actually stylish.

We did drink in the back of the limousine: Katie Williams, Joan Donning, Melissa Peake, and me, myself, and moi. Since it was Katie's car, we only had champagne. Then we could pretend we were actually upstanding people on our way to an upstanding luncheon where we would figure out how to save the world.

Melissa was some kind of broker or investment banker who only worked part-time. She always had something in her ear, and half the time, I couldn't tell if she was talking to us or to the thing in her ear. Katie was independently wealthy from some internet company she'd started when she was in her twenties, and Joan, well, Joan was in real estate. The market had tanked some time ago, however, so she hadn't been doing much.

I was the only one in the group who didn't actually work.

"How's Hayword's latest script?" Katie asked.

I glanced at Joan. She raised her eyebrows knowingly.

"All of his scripts are fine," I said. "He's doing great. Had a little run-in with the clap. Got it from me. You know from all the guys I fuck. I think he's about over it now, but it put him off sex for a little while. He was afraid I'd accuse him of screwing around on me because he knows I would kill him if he cheated on me."

"Really?" Melissa asked, leaning forward. "I had no idea. You two seem so . . . vanilla."

I grinned. "I'm kidding. Hayword has never had the clap. Neither have I. We are very . . . vanilla. I was trying to throw a little Neapolitan in there."

"Or mocha fudge," Joan said. "That would be good. With strawberries on top."

"Well, Ariel is looking forward to spending time with David this weekend," Katie said. "He's a good boy."

"Yes, he definitely doesn't take after his mother," I said.

"Hey, did you hear Dorothy and Peter Pritcher lost a child?" Melissa said. "Died in its sleep." She snapped her fingers. "Just like that. The police were going to investigate, but they figured out it was SIDS. So glad my kids are over that age."

Joan and Katie glanced at me. I didn't say anything.

Katie finally cleared her throat and said, "No, I hadn't heard. I should send them a condolence card."

I took a sip of champagne.

"What's wrong?" Melissa said. "What did I say?"

I didn't feel like explaining anything to this woman. I barely knew her. She'd been my neighbor for five or six years and we'd been to countless parties together, but that didn't mean anything. All I knew about her was that she liked to gossip and she was always on the phone.

"Someone said Dorothy had the baby blues psychosis," Melissa said, "so she could have smothered the kid. The police were being careful."

"Let's not talk about it," Joan said.

Melissa shrugged. "Yeah, it is sad."

I wanted to punch her.

Instead I drank more champagne.

Joan took my hand and held it, discreetly, between our legs. I let her. Her way of supporting me.

I stared out the window and drank.

By the time we got to the Shilton, I was three sheets to the wind. I didn't think anyone noticed.

We ordered appetizers first.

They brought us crackers with cheese on them. Or bruschetta. I never knew the difference. Melissa and Katie oohed and aahed over the little crackers. I looked down at them and something black fell onto my plate.

Melissa screamed. Or maybe it was Joan.

I leaned closer to the plate.

It was a fake eyelash. I looked up and around. Nobody here but us chickens. I felt my eye. Yep. One of mine was missing.

"Brooke!" Katie said.

"I know," I said. I pulled off the other one. "Phew. Now that feels much better."

The waitress was there now. She must have heard the scream.

"Here," I said.

She held out her palm and I dropped the false eyelashes on them. "Could you dispose of them properly, Miss? We wouldn't want them to end up in a land mine."

"Landfill," Katie said. She smiled at the waitress.

"What's that on your arm?" Melissa asked the waitress.

I tried to focus and see what she was seeing.

The waitress quickly pulled her sleeve down.

"I burned it," she said. "It's almost all healed. I'll take these now. Lunch will be here soon." The waitress left us.

Melissa leaned forward. "That's no burn. I bet she's got it."

"Got what?" Joan asked.

"You know," Melissa said. "You've heard about it. A lot of

the help, a lot of illegals, have this disease or rash or something. It's very contagious. Their skin gets really scaly or something. Someone told me she was at a restaurant and a piece of skin fell off into her food."

"I don't believe that," Joan said.

"That is complete horseshit," I said. "Only a complete asshole would believe that."

"Shhh," Katie said. "Brooke, you're talking very loudly."

"Okay, okay," I whispered. Or maybe I shouted.

"I thought you said she went to rehab." Melissa or Katie whispered that to Joan. Or to each other.

"That's what I heard," one of them said. "It doesn't always take."

"And a child is a he or a she," I said. "Not an 'it.' Do you know how devastated that mother must feel to have her baby die and then some little bitch like you talks about her smothering her baby? It's sick. Babies are not 'its'. You're an it. You're a shit."

Then I laughed.

Katie whispered something to Melissa. Or the other way around.

I kept smiling.

Joan asked me if I was all right.

I think I ate a lobster. I told the waitress I wanted to donate the empty lobster body to the poor. Melissa and Katie tried to figure out the seating chart for the Benefit. Then they all got up to go look at the ballroom.

I stayed seated.

"I'll wait for you here," I said.

I ordered another drink.

Then I called David's school and asked why they were scaring the shit out of my son with all the emergency drills.

"Are you drunk, Mrs. Lightman?" the principal asked.

"No, it's my allergy medicine," I said. "Hello? I can't hear you. Must be going through a tunnel." I turned the phone off.

I felt sick to my stomach.

I motioned to the waitress. "I'm not feeling well," I said. I'm sure she recognized the illness. "Could you please get me a room?" I handed her my credit card. "I want to go lie down for a bit."

A few minutes later, she came back with a keycard and my credit card.

"Do you want me to take you?" she asked.

I waved her away. "I'm fine, fine. Tell my friends they're a bunch of insensitive assholes, and I can't stand to be here with them any more."

"Do you really want me to tell them that?" she asked.

I wished I could see her face clearly. She was being quite kind to me.

"Naw," I said. "Tell them I wasn't feeling well, so I went home."

I stood up. I should not have worn high heels. Why the fuck did I ever wear them? Bad for the back and if I had to run for my life . . . well, I wouldn't be able to.

"Fourth floor," she said.

The waitress walked with me to the elevator.

"My little boy died," I said.

I could hear myself and I couldn't seem to stop myself.

"I'm so sorry," she said. She put her arm around my shoulders.

"No, it's okay," I said. "It's been almost ten years. He'd be ten this month if he'd lived."

"Still," she said. "It hurts. My brother has been gone for twelve years and I still miss him."

"Did he get to grow up?" I asked.

She shook her head.

"Ah, so you understand," I said. "They never got to grow

up. They never got to figure out if they were sinners or saints. Carpenters or preachers. Bellmen or bell-weathermen."

The elevator door opened. The waitress leaned in and pushed the "four" button. Then she stepped out. I think she had tears in her eyes. The doors shut.

"Fourth, fourth, fourth," I said. I looked at the keycard. It was difficult to read. Lucky this hotel wrote the room number on the little envelope they put the keycard in.

The elevator doors opened. I felt like I was going to throw up. I could barely walk.

"I need a fucking drink," I said.

I walked down the hallway.

It was a long hallway.

I thought I saw a rabbit running down it.

Or was that a man coming toward me?

Oh fuck. He was going to rob me.

No. He had white hair. And a beard and mustache. How many white-haired robbers were there?

"Brooke? Is that you?"

I recognized the voice. Could barely see his face.

"Greg," I said. I slapped his chest with my hand. "Greg Douglas as I live and burn. How are you? I am not fine. My lunch, liquid as it was, did not agree with me. I had lobster, too, or some kind of thing that is not happy in my stomach." I laughed. "But I can't find my room. What are you doing here?"

"Your room is right down here," he said.

He put his arm around my waist and walked with me down the hall. Then he took the keycard and opened the door. At least that was what I thought happened. I didn't really know. I went into the bathroom and threw up. That felt better. Somehow I got into bed, got all the way under the covers, and I fell to sleep.

Either that or I blacked out.

SEVEN

I woke up with a throbbing headache. The blinds were closed, but I could tell it was still daylight. I threw off the covers and sat up.

I heard someone talking in the other room.

I got out of bed, straightened my dress, ran my fingers through my hair, and then walked into the other room.

Greg Douglas was standing in the middle of the room talking on the phone. He waved at me and smiled. He was still as beautiful as he had been when I had last seen him—nine years ago? He and his wife Lizzie had attended the same grief counseling group for parents that Hayword and I attended for a while. Greg and I often pretended to go out for a smoke, and then we'd sit in the courtyard talking. Sometimes we shared a drink from a flask one of us had. We hadn't seen each other often, but I had always thought he was a good guy, a strong guy. He could sift through bullshit and see the truth, something Hayword was not very good at, as far as I was concerned.

Lizzie and Greg had always seemed like normal people even though they were in the business. She did editing, and he was a cameraman. They never talked about work. The four of us had gone out for coffee a couple times after the group. I don't remember what we talked about, but it wasn't about the biz.

Maybe we talked about our children, dead and alive.

Lizzie had the saddest smile.

I had never taken Greg to the love nest.

Of course, back then, I didn't have the love nest.

Too bad.

But then again, he was married.

I did not dabble in married men.

I went back into the bedroom. I got my purse and went into the bathroom. I brushed my hair, dabbed my eyes. Looked in the mirror.

I wasn't drunk any more, but I was still a bit high.

What a scene I must have made.

I hoped Hayword never found out.

I went into the other room.

Greg hung up the hotel phone.

"I ordered some seltzer," he said. "And soup. Crackers."

I sat in one of the chairs. He sat opposite of me.

"My hero," I said. "I always suspected you were a knight in shining armor."

He laughed.

"It's good to see you," he said.

"Yeah, well, I'm sorry you had to see me this way," I said. "It was stupid. I was in the car with a bunch of women and one of them was talking about someone whose baby had died and she was so stupid and ignorant and I wanted to punch her or kill her or crash the car. Something. Instead, I sat there and drank."

He nodded. "I know. Sometimes something little sends me into a tailspin. I still miss him so much."

I pulled my feet up underneath me. "There's no one I can talk to about it. I went to rehab for a while and they said I had trouble because of Alberto's death and I thought that was so stupid. They didn't understand. I'm not having *trouble* because he died. I am a completely different person because he died. And I won't be the person I was before because I stop drinking. Because he'll still be dead."

Greg nodded. "I hear ya."

"How's Lizzie doing?" I asked.

He shook his head. "I don't know. We don't talk any more. We divorced about eight years ago."

"I'm sorry," I said.

"No, it was good. She remarried and had a couple more kids. I've got Suzanne, you know, from my first marriage. But Leonard was Lizzie's only child. She wasn't going to get any more from me. So it worked out. How's Hayword and the kids?"

"Hayword's still Hayword," I said. "No different. David will be a teen soon. I dread that. Fern is grown and in college, getting her master's degree in psychology. She still is not very fond of me."

Greg laughed. "Mothers and daughters," he said. "That's always a tricky thing. I bet David adores you."

"David is a good kid," I said. "He's older than his years in some ways and younger in other ways."

Greg nodded. "Yep. Suzanne still likes her dad, but we don't see each other often. She's living in Chicago now."

"Is that where you moved after you left here?" I asked.

"No, we went to New York for a while," he said. "Then we divorced and Lizzie came back here. I can get more work out here so I came back, too. It's only been a couple of years." He shrugged. "I'm getting used to it again. Kind of isolating. I don't always notice."

I laughed. Maybe I giggled.

I had an instant crush on this man.

Maybe I had had a crush all of those years ago. Most of the time I didn't like people to know about Alberto. Well, I didn't want them to know he was dead. They looked at me differently after they knew. Treated me differently. But Greg had always known. And I had always known about his loss. And how he took it. It wasn't good what had happened to his son, but he wasn't going to let it ruin his life. It didn't make him better or more saintly if it ruined his life.

Shit happens and you move on.

That was my motto, too.

I was sure it was my motto.

I rubbed my face.

At least I wanted that to be my motto.

I had moved on. My life was completely different from before Alberto died.

Completely.

Almost completely different.

"Gawd, I want a drink," I said.

Someone knocked on the door. Greg got up and answered it. I didn't even watch him go. I let him take care of it. How refreshing. Hayword was always asking me what he should do. Always asking me what I wanted.

Don't ask me! Just fucking do it!

Only make certain it's what I want you to do.

I heard the door shut. Greg came back into the living room. He set a tray on the table in front of me. On it was a plate of crackers, butter, grapes. A bowl of soup. And a glass of bubbly.

Bubbly seltzer.

Greg sat across from me again.

I took a sip of the seltzer. Then I got a cracker and chewed on it.

"Dig in," I said.

"I'm good," he said.

I laughed. I wasn't even sure why it was funny.

"Man, it's great to see you," I said. "I feel like I've been in a cage, and now I see you and the cage feels open. I'm not even sure why."

"We come from the same clan," he said. "We bear the same scars. So we know each other. We don't need words."

I felt like I was going to cry.

But I didn't.

"How long was I asleep?" I asked.

"A few hours," he said. "I went downstairs and had lunch and came back up and you were still sleeping. I decided to stay and make sure you're all right."

"You don't have to stay now," I said. "I'm okay."

He smiled. "You don't seem okay. You got an anniversary coming up?"

I nodded. "Alberto's birthday. I don't know why every year it's such a surprise to me." I sighed. "I better call home. They're going to be worried about me."

"He nodded and stood up.

"Don't go," I said. "I'll call in the other room. I'll be right back."

"All right," he said.

I got up and went into the bedroom. I pulled my phone from my purse.

Damn. About twenty messages and texts. I didn't listen to or read them. I called Hayword.

"Where are you?" he answered. "I've been worried sick."

"I'm sorry," I said. "I wasn't feeling well so I got a hotel room here."

"Joan and Katie said you disappeared," he said.

"Yeah, well, I'm fine," I said. "Are you still in the city? I need a ride home."

"No," he said. "I came home early. Thought I'd take you all out for pizza."

"You go ahead," I said. "Take Eartha, too."

"She's already started dinner," he said. "She's amazing. Hardly spent any money and she's making this feast for us. You want me to call a car for you?"

"No," I said. "I'll call in a bit." I started to tell him that I'd run into Greg Douglas. It was on the tip of my tongue. But then I didn't. Not sure why.

Not sure why I wanted to tell him in the first place.

"You really all right?" Hayword asked. "They said you were a little . . . tipsy."

Goddamn women. Bet it was Katie. Laying the groundwork to fuck my husband.

"I'm fine," I said. "I'll be home in a while."

"You're not spending the night there are you?"

He knew I wouldn't do that. David got a little upset if I didn't come home every night. We thought my stint at rehab would have cured him of it, but it hadn't. We'd taken him to therapists. They hadn't been sure what was going on. David didn't care if Hayword was gone. But I had to spend the night at home.

"No," I said. "I'll be home. Have a good dinner."

I went back into the living room. Greg looked up as I came into the room. He smiled.

I couldn't get over how beautiful he was.

I couldn't see any scars.

I sat across from him again. We talked for a while. He told me about the first baseball game Leonard had played. Talked about all the hours they had spent together practicing because Leonard was so nervous about playing in front of people.

For some reason, it wasn't painful listening to him. Even when he talked about the day Leonard died. And then I was talking about Alberto. About how different he had been from both of my other children. Fern had growled coming out of my womb. David was colicky and he cried a lot.

Alberto cooed. Seemed so happy. Blissful. I liked sitting in the room with him. Being in the room with him.

He was such a happy baby that I never felt guilty when I left him. Like when Hayword and I went out for dinner. David had always cried when we went away, and babysitters hated that.

Alberto was happy when we left and happy when we came home. Fern was twelve years old, so we let her babysit him and David. She insisted she was old enough. We were certain she was right.

When we came home that night, Alberto was fine. In the morning, he was no longer alive.

Fern screamed so long and so loud that her father slapped her. He was afraid she was going to pass out.

David was too young to understand. He was less than two years older than his brother. But he cried.

I didn't remember what I did or said. Did I cry? Did I curl up into a ball?

We tried to resuscitate Alberto. Hayword called 911, and they told him how to do CPR on an infant.

Greg listened to all of this and nodded.

At the grief group, they had wanted us to talk. But it was excruciating. I didn't want to relive the most horrible thing that had ever happened to us. Some of the people kept telling the stories of their children's deaths over and over.

At least it seemed that way.

It didn't help me to hear what they said. It seemed like every week I learned new, surprising, and horrible ways that children could die. I'd hurry home and examine my children for signs of anything untoward.

I didn't go to the grief group very often. Hayword went for a while.

We sent Fern to a therapist for a time. She blamed herself because she had been babysitting him.

I told her, "He was fine when we got home. You didn't have anything to do with it. He just died."

She screamed, "It's all your fault! You should have known I couldn't handle it!"

I nodded. Of course it was my fault. In Fern's mind, everything was my fault.

Where had I gone wrong?

I said all of this out loud to Greg.

"Lizzie thought it was my fault," he said. "She even said it was my fault a couple of times when we were fighting. She is pretty religious. She thought God punished us when we didn't behave. I said if God killed children because their parents did something wrong, then he was an asshole."

"Exactly!" I said. "I remember hearing something on talk radio soon after Alberto died. This man's son had died, and the talk show host told the man he should consider what sins he had committed and he should repent so god would forgive him. I started swearing at the radio. 'Fuck you, god! Fuck you, god!' I thought if I'm being punished for some supposed sin to get me to change my ways, it wasn't going to work. I was going to do whatever I wanted to do. No invisible being in the sky was going to force me to live a certain way."

"That's right."

"Of course I heard this radio thing a few months after the house had burned down. So I had been starting to wonder what the hell was going on. First my son dies and then my house burns down. The house burning down didn't compare. In fact, I hardly noticed it. It was a good excuse to move. But my family was traumatized. Fern asked me what we were being punished for. I don't know where she got that. We never took them to church, so guilt must be in the air."

"That's tough," he said. "When did that happen?"

"A few months after you left," I said. "It was all the talk of Brentwood. The house could have been salvaged. In fact the insurance company wanted to rebuild. Our lawyers worked some magic so that we could leave. It was amazingly freeing to leave the house and almost everything we owned and move away from the city. I really thought my life was going to change."

"And did it?" he asked.

"Sure," I said. "In some ways."

I looked at him. I wanted to tell him everything.

And nothing.

He knew my son had died, but that was not a stain on me. That wasn't anything horrible I had done. It was something awful that had happened to my son and to my family.

All the other stuff, well, that was all on me.

I looked at this man and I wanted to be in his arms. I knew he could comfort me. I was absolutely certain of it. He knew. He understood.

He was separate from me. I looked at him and didn't feel like I had to take care of him.

I didn't feel as though I had to take care of any of the people I brought to the love nest either. Oh crap. Now *I* was thinking of it as the love nest. If I started to feel responsible for my lovers or how they felt, then I ended it. I imagined I would never have to worry about Greg Douglas, yet he would take care of me.

Not that I needed anyone to take care of me.

But wouldn't that be nice? For an instant. A day. A week.

I had been responsible for the care and feeding of Hayword and my family since I was . . . a child, really. And I had failed so miserably. I had failed in the worst way possible: One of my children had died.

But Greg Douglas knew.

He knew it wasn't my fault.

I sighed and leaned back in the chair.

What was wrong with me?

I wanted to keep this man. I wanted to walk into the bedroom and be in his arms. Have him tell me it was going to be all right.

Suddenly I felt dizzy. The room seemed to be trembling.

I glanced at the curtains. They were moving. That meant it wasn't me: It was an earthquake.

I heard rattling. Things falling.

Greg and I both stood. That didn't help. The hotel was swaying. I tried to remember what I was supposed to do in case of an earthquake. I'd been through enough of them in the twenty years or so I'd lived in California. I should remember.

I bet David remembered.

Greg grabbed my arm and took me to the table behind the couch, near the bar. We got underneath it.

"I'm not sure this is sturdy enough," Greg said. "But it'll have to do."

We were so close to each other that I could smell him.

Funny, I didn't want to fuck him. I wanted to smell him. I liked being this close and smelling his smell.

Hadn't there been a time when I had felt that way about Hayword?

Goddamn it. I was tired of Hayword popping into my brain.

The swaying stopped. We slowly got up from underneath the table.

The lights were off.

I looked around the room.

Didn't look like much damage.

"5.4 I'd guess," Greg said.

"That was a 6.0 I bet."

I picked up the phone. No dial tone.

We went to the window, Greg opened the blinds, and we

looked down at the street. Cars were stopped out front. I saw broken glass on the sidewalk. The street looked like it had buckled a bit. I had never seen that before. I heard car horns blaring. In the distance, I heard sirens.

"I better call home," I said.

I got my cell phone. No service.

I felt a little panicky. I needed to know everyone was all right. I couldn't be off someplace drunk, with a strange man, and find out someone in my family was hurt. I didn't think even I could come back from that.

"Greg, I want to go downstairs to see if I can get service," I said.

Greg took out his phone. "Mine's working," he said. He handed it to me.

I couldn't remember anyone's phone number. Except the house phone.

I tried that. The phone rang.

Eartha answered.

"Is everyone all right?" I asked. "Did you feel it there?"

"Yes, we're all fine," she said. "I think. Hayword slipped coming down the stairs."

"I'm fine!" I heard Hayword's voice in the background.

"Here's David," Eartha said.

"Mom!" David. "It was so cool. I knew exactly what to do. The wind was really howling. Did you notice? Just before."

The Santa Ana winds no doubt. They'd been off and on for weeks. Driving some people crazy. I had hardly noticed them.

"And then the ground was shaking," he said. "I thought a tree had fallen on the house. I told everyone to get under the kitchen table."

"Everyone as in Dad and Eartha?"

"Yep," he said. "Dad slipped on the bottom step, but he's okay. You gonna be here soon?"

"It'll probably be late," I said. "I don't know if I can get a car."

"Okay," David said. He didn't even sound afraid. "Love you!"

He must have handed the phone to his father.

"Hi, Brooke," Hayword said. "You all right."

"Yep," I said. "You hurt your foot?"

"I twisted my ankle a bit coming down the stairs. It's starting to swell. It's my right leg. I don't think I can drive to come get you. Should I ask Eartha?"

"No," I said. "I wouldn't send a newbie to downtown Los Angeles after an earthquake. I'll try to get a limo."

"I don't know if they'll come out this far," he said.

"I'll figure out something," I said. "Keep in touch."

I handed the phone back to Greg.

"I wonder if the electricity is out all over town," Greg said. "I've got to be on the job in about an hour. Maybe I'll have the night off. Well, maybe not." He looked down at his phone. "Nope. Studio is fine." He looked up at me. "I guess I better get going. You all right? You have a way home?"

"Sure," I said. "I'm fine."

"What were you doing here anyway?" he asked. "Not that it's any of my business."

I smiled. "We're organizing the Benefit here on Saturday," I said. "Tying up loose ends while tying one on."

He smiled. "You always were very funny." He said it, but he was not laughing.

"I've got a ticket to that benefit," he said.

"Oh good," I said. "So I'll see you on Saturday?"

"I wasn't actually going to come," he said. "But maybe I will now."

I felt a nice little tickle in my stomach over this news.

"Good," I said.

I got my purse and the two of us went into the hallway—dark except for the emergency lights. We walked down the stairs together until we got to the lobby. People were milling around, inside and outside of the hotel.

Greg and I embraced. I wanted to keep a hold of him, but I let him go. I watched him walk away.

I felt like I had finally met the man of my dreams.

Or gotten reacquainted with the man of my dreams.

I went to the desk and asked if they could call me a limo to take me home, or a taxi, anything with wheels. The man at the desk said he doubted he could get anything, but he'd try.

It was almost dark outside.

I heard a click as the electricity came back on. People cheered.

I wished I could go back upstairs to bed.

They tried to get a car for me. I called Hayword, and he tried to get a car for me. I tried to get a car for me.

Nobody could come.

"This is Los Angeles, for chrissakes," I said. "We know earthquakes."

"David's getting a little nervous," Hayword said. "He doesn't think you'll be able to get home. The winds have whipped up one of the fires, by the way. He's worried it's going to get all the way here."

"Will it?" I asked.

"I doubt it," Hayword said. "The closest one is two canyons away, I think."

"Let me try to figure something out," I said. "I'll call later."

Crap, crap, crap.

I paced the lobby. How was I going to get home?

Got a text. "You okay?" Mark.

"Stuck at the Shilton," I texted back. "No car." This was the last time I went anywhere without my own damn car.

"Be there in thirty."

"No. I'll be fine."

"What about David?"

Shit. Had I told Mark about having to be home for David? I thought I never told him anything. Yesterday being the exception, of course.

"On my way," he texted.

I went to the restaurant and asked for a sandwich. The electricity hadn't been out long enough to put my life in jeopardy by eating any of their food, plus I thought it was a good idea. I'd thrown up everything I'd eaten for lunch. Time to fill up again.

I took the sandwich up to my room. Ate it. Then washed up. Tried to make myself look like I wasn't the whore of Babylon.

I looked at myself in the mirror.

"Well, maybe the older sister of the whore of Babylon."

Oh, who was I kidding? I looked like a two-dollar hooker.

If there was such a thing.

Or I would be if I were any place besides Los Angeles or New York.

Or Mexico City.

Or . . . shut up!

I went downstairs to the lobby. I felt too tarted up.

What the fuck was wrong with me? I was seldom embarrassed about anything.

That was my fucking charm.

People in the lobby were talking about the earthquake. I could still hear sirens outside. Wondered if anyone was hurt. They had the news on in the bar. A dozen or more people stood watching.

I went outside.

It was now night.

A few minutes later a blue electric or hybrid car drove up to the hotel. I heard a honk. I looked around. Then looked down.

It was Mark.

I walked over to the blue car, opened the door, and got in.

"Did you have any trouble?" I asked.

He quickly pulled away from the curb.

"Traffic is a nightmare," he said. "But I can get us through it."

"Thanks, Mark," I said. "You're a lifesaver."

I glanced at him. He looked good, as usual. Dressed in jeans and a shirt.

"Were you out?" I asked. "You look nice."

"Went over to a friend's house," he said. "For dinner."

"Did you already eat?" I asked. "It's barely six."

He didn't say anything.

"Did you blow off dinner on my account?" I asked. "Christ, Mark. Why would you do that?"

"It was a set-up," he said. "They had some women they wanted me to meet. Or woman. Supposed to be a dinner party, but it was mostly my two friends and a bunch of women and myself. I was glad to get out of there."

I laughed. "Oh shit, Mark. Your friends are going to be pissed."

"I have the earthquake as an excuse," he said. "Everyone needs a plumber after an earthquake. How was your day?"

I laughed. "You have no idea." I started to tell him about Greg. And then I realized he wasn't my goddamn girlfriend. He was my fucking partner. My lover. I shouldn't be telling him about my knight in shining armor. Or whatever Greg Douglas was.

"Did you like any of the women?" I asked.

I didn't pay attention to where he was going or what he was doing. I only knew we weren't stopping, which was good. If he saw a flashing light or a traffic slow-up, he made a U-turn or went down another street.

I enjoyed competent men.

"Sure," he said. "They all seemed nice. I've never had trouble finding women, Brooke. I'm not looking for anyone else. I'm happy with you."

I made a noise. "How is that even possible?" Oops. There I was. Speaking my thoughts out loud again. "Oh, wait, I know. You're not really interested in a long term relationship either."

"No, that's not it," he said.

"You knew I wasn't available from the very start," I said. "We talked about it. You said that was fine with you."

"I know," he said. "I'm still fine with it. *You* keep bringing it up."

"I do?" I looked out the window. Really? "Why did you call me, you know, last February? I mean, you said you've never gone after a married woman before. But you called me. You asked me if we could see each other. Why?"

Usually I was forward with the men or women I wanted. But I hadn't said anything to Mark. I hadn't thought about him that way. I mean, he had worked in my house. It seemed tacky to lust after the handyman.

Although I did love handy men.

Oh gawd.

"It was the way you looked at me when we talked," he said. "You listened to me. You seemed to respect my opinion. You didn't treat me like the help or like someone you wanted to fuck. That's usually what I encounter: People who don't really see me, or people who want to get something from me, either a deal— money wise—or sex. You didn't do any of that. You seemed so real. And then I saw you with your husband and something changed in you. You were a completely different person. I didn't want that person. I wanted the person you were when you were with me."

"And which person did you get?"

He didn't say anything for a moment. Then he said, "A little of both. Except some days I get a lot of you. Like yesterday."

"Too much blathering on yesterday," I said.

"So did you have a good day?" he asked. "At your meeting for the Benefit?"

He knew my schedule?

"What, are you my stalker? How'd you know about that?"

He laughed. "You told me," he said. "You tell me things. I pay attention."

"Well, stop it," I said. "The meeting was horrible. And things have started to bother me." I shook my head. "Must be the Santa Anas, or the fires, or the earthquake. Or the stupid zombie movie. They've conned me into rewriting a zombie movie. A fucking zombie movie. Can you imagine? They want me to make it sexy."

Mark laughed. "A zombie movie? Never saw a zombie anyone would want to have sex with."

"That's what I said! For some reason I agreed to do it. Hayword seems to have his heart set on it. Thinks it'll change the world."

Mark glanced at me.

"Yes, he's fucking delusional," I said.

"Maybe you could make it fun," he said. "Or funny."

"I never wanted this life," I said.

"What?"

We were on the freeway now. It was pretty jammed up.

"You never wanted to write scripts?" he asked.

"I never wanted the Hollywood life," I said. "I don't know how it happened. I guess I let it. Everybody says they want to be rich and famous: I never did. I don't mind the writing part. Just all the other stuff. I mean, who the fuck is real here? What is real here? I can't tell. Sometimes I feel like I'm living a really bad movie. Or a really good one. I'm not sure."

"What kind of life did you want to live?" he asked.

I shrugged. "I don't know," I said. "I wanted Hayword and me to be happy. Maybe run a regional theater. I wanted us raise our children. Have nothing bad happen. I've never been extraordinary, and you have to be extraordinary out here or else you disappear. I feel like I've disappeared." I closed my eyes and leaned back against the car seat. "Maybe have a little bar or restaurant or something, by the beach. People I love coming and going. People I'm comfortable with. I'm never comfortable, Mark. Everyone and everything makes me nervous. What about you? You wanted to be a chef?"

"I wanted a family," he said. "I figured we'd each have our jobs—my wife and I—but the primary focus would be our family. I knew pretty early on I wasn't going to be a chef. A cook maybe, but not a chef. But even that would have been difficult. I'm good at what I do now. People need my services. I can pay my bills. That feels nice. Worrying about a restaurant? Naw, I don't think so. Not unless it was really easygoing."

I glanced over at him. "Maybe I should let you cook for me. I don't give a shit about food, you know. Although lately Eartha has been making some really good dishes."

"Who is this Eartha, anyway?"

"She's the homeless person Hayword let move into our garden house," I said. "So far it's been going all right. Why'd you and your wife break up anyway?"

"It doesn't matter," he said. "We didn't work out."

"Come on," I said. "I've spilled my guts to you."

"She was cheating on me," he said. "And she fell in love with the guy."

"Did you ever cheat on her?" I asked.

"No, never," he said. "I've always been a monogamous guy."

"You shouldn't waste your monogamy on me," I said. "If

you knew who I really was, if you knew all the things I'd done, you wouldn't want to have anything to do with me."

"I know who you really are," he said.

I shook my head and looked out the window. Then I closed my eyes and leaned back again.

I opened my eyes when Mark stopped the car. I looked around. I was home. I must have fallen asleep.

"Thank you," I said to him. "Do you want the key to the studio? You could sleep there. I could come by tomorrow."

"No, thanks," he said. "I've got a job in the morning. I'll see you Monday."

"You okay?" I asked. I felt like I should say something. "Was your mom's place okay in the earthquake? Your son's?"

He nodded. "Everyone's fine. Go on in and be with your family."

I looked at the house. The car rocked a little from the wind. I leaned toward him to kiss him. He put his hand on my arm.

"No," he said. "You better not."

I looked at him. What had happened? Something had changed.

"What's wrong?" I asked.

He shook his head. "Nothing," he said. "We'll talk about it later. Go on."

"Fuck 'em and leave 'em," I said. "That's your MO. I understand. I'll see you later."

He smiled. But he was not laughing.

I got out of the car and went into the house. Eartha, David, and Hayword sat at the kitchen table playing Scrabble. David looked relieved when he saw me: His whole body relaxed.

"Hi, Mom. You wanna play Scrabble?"

I wanted to say no. I wanted to go to sleep. Hide under the covers. Run away. Go away. Do away.

But I went to the table and sat next to Eartha. She smiled.

Then she put her arm across my shoulder, as a way to welcome me, I supposed. It was gentle, it was quick, but not too quick. I leaned into it, although I doubted she noticed. It was exactly what I needed at that moment. A human touch. A human touch from someone I hadn't fucked, disappointed, screwed over, or otherwise harmed.

Now that was her one great thing for the day.

EIGHT

We felt a couple of aftershocks during the night but nothing major.

In the morning, Hayword's ankle wasn't any better. I suggested he go in for an X-ray.

"I'll drive you," I said. Once again I was up at the crack of dawn.

"No," he said. "I want you to read the script."

"I can read it in the doctor's office."

"Go to your studio," he said. "Or stay here. I don't care. Get takeout. Make a day of it. I want you to be able to concentrate. Eartha can take me. Then she can drive me to work. I won't stay long and she'll get to tool around town. She said she wanted to check out some places."

I shrugged. "Hey, trying to do my wifely duty. I really have no desire to sit in a doctor's office with you."

"I knew that," he said. "You didn't need to say that out loud."

"Didn't know I did."

After the three of them left and the house was empty, except for me, I went upstairs into my office. I stood and looked around. It seemed cold, unused, stuffy. I opened the window. It was too chilly out. I closed it again. Then I picked up the manuscript.

"*Zombie Town,*" I said out loud as I looked down at the first page. I shook my head.

I tucked the script under my arm, went out to the car, and drove to my bungalow.

The house seemed different today. Felt lived in. I could still smell Mark. Or the two of us. I went into the bedroom. The bed was still unmade. Guess the cleaning lady hadn't been in yet.

I straightened the sheets and covers. Then I went to the kitchen and opened the patio door a bit. I sat at the table and started to read *Zombie Town*.

It went quicker than I thought it would. I groaned but not as much as I thought I would. The zombies were actually aliens from another planet. They had destroyed their own environment which had let loose a plague that caused the people of that planet to become the living dead with an insatiable desire to feast on human blood. Well, first they wanted to feast on each other's blood, but they soon ran out of candidates, so before someone was the last person on that planet, they decided to invade another planet: Earth.

A band of heroes—made up of men and women of different ethnicities—tried to save Earth from the zombies. In the end they succeeded in blowing up the zombie ship, but more ships were on their way.

Boys would like this movie. Lots of shit blowing up. Lots of aliens eating people. Good times.

How was I going to make this movie sexy?

I put the script down. I looked at my phone. Maybe if I had some sex, I could make it sexy.

I started to text Mark. Then I threw the phone across the room because I knew I would be too lazy to get up and get it.

I was not calling him. I should be thinking of ways to break up with him, not get him to come over. I had every intention of hooking up with Greg Douglas at the Benefit tomorrow. I rarely kept two lovers (and a husband) at the same time. That was too much juggling even for me, so I would have to get rid of Mark. Or never start with Greg.

And he seemed too perfect to resist.

I thought about calling Sally St. James. Not to have sex with her but to ask what her ideas were for sexing up the script.

No. I wouldn't do that either. She'd have me smoking her cigarettes for her again.

I opened my laptop and got the "Zombie Town" file Hayword had e-mailed me. I stared at the screen.

How could I get people to care about zombies?

Someone in the movie would have to care about zombies.

Someone cute would have to care about a cute zombie.

There were no cute zombies.

Beauty was in the eye of the beholder.

Remember *Beauty and the Beast.*

I selected "Zombie Town" on the title page and began typing over it: "Beauty and the Zombie."

I leaned back in the chair.

Maybe the aliens who come to Earth have a plague which distorts their looks so they look like the undead to humans. Humans are afraid of them—they are afraid of catching the zombie plague. But the zombies also look like humans, except they have the plague, so they are probably some kind of human cousin.

The zombies could come in teeth blazing to eat everyone or they could do it the American way: Hire (or acquire) a good PR person. Or have an attractive zombie leader.

I looked around the room. What could his name be? I glanced

at an old newspaper on the coffee table. The lead story was written by a Dennis Thomas.

Thomas. That was a good normal name for an alien. He's got the plague, but he's a good-looking *normal* guy.

How could a character be undead and still be good-looking?

I remembered Melissa mentioning yesterday at lunch that there was some kind of skin disease plaguing the migrant workers.

"That can't be real," I said. "Just more anti-immigrant bullshit."

I googled "skin disease migrants." Scanned the list of articles popping up. Clicked on one.

"You're kidding," I said. Melissa hadn't been completely wrong. There was some kind of peculiar skin disease that was considered contagious and a bit disfiguring. The CDC hadn't figured out what was causing it yet or how to stop it. It was more prevalent in the migrant populations and amongst the poor.

I shook my head. Truth was always stranger than fiction.

"The zombies have a mysterious skin disease," I said. "That'll work."

I got up and opened the living room curtains. I rarely did that. It was such a beautiful day, though. I wanted the light. The sky was blue. I saw no signs of the fires. I could see the trees outside moving to the wind, but it didn't seem too wicked. A nice breeze came through the partially open patio door.

I almost felt peaceful. Again. Third time in so many days.

I typed up my ideas so far.

What next?

What would Thomas, the alien leader, do? He's a smart good-looking alien. He decides to find a scientist sympathetic to his cause. Instead of saying "take me to your leader," he says, "take me to your leading exobiologist." They take him to a group of scientists and he notices a female scientist who seems a little shy, a little out of place.

I smiled. Okay. Now I had a love story.

What could her name be?

I knew immediately. Colleen. I liked the name. It was a good Irish name. It would go with McMurphy. I remembered Colleen McMurphy from the TV show *China Beach.* She'd been a nurse in Vietnam. She was always falling in love with the wrong guy. She was strong and fucked up. Always admired her.

I thought about typing in Colleen McMurphy.

I shook my head. No, then I'd keep seeing my Colleen as the *China Beach* Colleen—Dana Delany. My Colleen had light brown hair. She might even be blond. Wears glasses. Doesn't care about makeup or clothes. She cares about saving the world and protecting it from Menace with a capital "M."

I laughed.

Wouldn't it be great to actually be able to protect the world— or anyone—from Menace with a capital "M."

Colleen Kelly. That was her name. She didn't drink. She didn't go out with bad men. She was sensible and smart.

I started typing as I was thinking. "Colleen and Thomas hit it off right away. She's suspicious of him, but he assures her the zombie aliens have come to Earth in peace. After a while, the audience won't notice his skin disease—his zombie disease. He's so kind to Colleen. He encourages her to take blood and tissue samples from him and any of his fellow aliens. She'll discover they are not contagious.

"'There are some bad aliens,' Thomas tells Colleen. Those are the ones where the plague has gone to their brains and they can't help themselves. 'I thought Earthlings were compassionate,' he says. 'But your people keep killing us. It is a sickness we have. We've come to this planet for your wisdom, so that we can learn to take care of our planet better, to follow your lead.'"

I laughed and shook my head. "Poor girl. She doesn't have a chance."

I continued typing.

"Colleen and Thomas spend a great deal of time together. All of her tests indicate that the zombie plague is not transferable from the aliens to the humans. Colleen falls in love with Thomas. They make passionate love. She defends the zombie aliens to anyone who will listen. She cites scientific proof that they are harmless. She kisses Thomas on camera.

"Soon zombies are popular all over the planet. Celebrities are seen with their favorite zombie alien. They're all the rage.

"Then one morning Colleen wakes up and her skin has started to change. Soon there is no denying it: She has the plague and so do many others. She is a pariah amongst her colleagues—and all around the world. She's called the zombie traitor. She realizes Thomas duped her. She should have never trusted him. She asks him why he did this to her. He says he knew that with her help they could spread the plague all over the planet. Unlike the aliens, humans could pass on the plague by touch or through the air, and the plague was terminal for them. He laughs and says she was so easy and so stupid.

"Colleen is devastated. She has to hide from everyone. She works tirelessly to find a cure for the human zombies. Colleen becomes a zombie in looks, but she has no desire to eat human flesh. Only the humans who get it from humans eat other humans. Since she got the plague from Thomas, she has no thirst for human blood or appetite for human brains."

I laughed. It was almost fun to be so ridiculous.

"Human brains. Hah!"

I glanced out the window. Some guy in a dirty business suit was walking by. If he'd held his arms out straight, he'd have the zombie look down.

I stared at my screen and started typing again.

"While the human zombies devour one another, the zombie aliens begin taking over planet Earth. They are using up the planet's resources faster than humans have been. The weather changes drastically. The air and water are choked with pollution. Colleen finds another scientist and they go on the run."

I looked around the room. What would the other scientist's name be? I could name her after Melissa who told me about the zombie skin condition. No. I wouldn't want her to think I was honoring her. Marissa. She'd have the zombie plague, too, but she got it from an alien so she doesn't want to eat people either. Or maybe she does. Probably the studio will want to change her to a man so the man and Colleen can have heterosexual sex. And then he can try to eat her. Her brains, that is. And Colleen would have to kill him. I shrugged. If they asked us to do that, maybe I would.

Although in the end, the studio would have the final say anyway.

I typed, "Colleen and Marissa run from the aliens and the human zombies. Eventually they stop trying to find an antidote. They're too ill. They're not willing to be captured or eaten, so they decide they'll drive over the Grand Canyon, homage *Thelma and Louise*. Just before they go over the cliff, they stop the car. Colleen wants to watch the sun come up one more time."

I stopped. I suddenly remembered when I was a kid I used to like getting up at sunrise. I'd go outside and watch the world change from gray to gold, watch the sun light sparkle on the dew on the grass. It was so quiet, except for the bird songs and my own breathing. Me breathing with the world. And I'd walk on the damp grass, barefoot, let the dew and the grass tickle my feet while the sun warmed my face. It was utterly peaceful.

I continued typing. "Colleen wants to feel the earth beneath her bare feet like she used to do when she was a kid, one more time. Both women take off their shoes and feel the dirt under their soles. They watch the sun come up, even though the light hurts their eyes. This connection with the earth and the light of the sun at the same time causes a chemical reaction in their bodies which instantly kills the plague."

I laughed. It was a little deus ex machina, but the simple and easy solutions were often the best solutions. In *The Day of the Triffids,* water killed the human-devouring plants. In *War of the Worlds,* it was a human virus. In *The Blob,* it was the cold.

"Colleen and Marissa are cured," I wrote. "They send out messages via short wave radio to people all over the world. Soon all the humans are cured. And because the zombie aliens can't stand the light, the humans have an advantage. The aliens are soon all killed or incarcerated. Colleen gets to watch Thomas hauled off to indefinite detention in chains. She shouts after him, 'I never loved you.' When he's out of earshot, he whispers, 'I wish I never loved you.' The last shot of the movie is of Colleen watching another sunrise. We see her back, first, and then the camera pans around to her front, where the audience sees that she is very pregnant—and she looks very afraid. The End."

I smiled. Sally St. James would love the last shot of *Beauty and the Zombie.*

"Always leave an opening for a sequel," I said.

I saved the document, wrote a quick e-mail to Hayword and Sally, and then I sent it off. If they liked it, I'd write the dialogue. Or maybe Hayword and I would write the dialogue. Just like old times.

I suddenly felt chilled. I got up and closed and locked the patio door. Then I pulled the living room drapes together.

I wished I had gotten Greg Douglas's number yesterday. I wanted to talk to him again.

Excitement was a red flag, I reminded myself. This had happened before and it wasn't good.

I looked at my phone. Joan had texted me. "You okay? Didn't

you say Violeta was visiting her mom in Mex? Saw her yesterday in L.A. as we were leaving."

I texted back, "I'm fine. Couldn't be V. She's in Mex."

Unless she lied to me for some reason.

I called her house.

It rang and rang. No answer. Of course she could be screening her calls.

I tried her cell phone. It went straight to voice mail.

Joan had probably been drunk.

My phone vibrated. I looked at it. Joan again. "Melissa P is such an asshole, BTW. Wanna get dressed together tomorrow? I've got a room at the Shilton."

I laughed. I texted her back. "As long as MP isn't invited. Don't want to see her naked talking on the bluetooth. Horrors."

"You drive. 5ish."

"You bet your ass I'm driving," I texted.

Hayword texted me his ankle was slightly sprained, and he was supposed to keep it elevated for a day. No dancing allowed.

I knew what that meant: I was going to the Benefit alone.

That was absolutely all right with me.

I got takeout at some fast food hovel, ate it quickly in the car, then threw the wrapping out so David wouldn't see any evidence of it. I figured I should set a better example for him, especially now that Eartha was feeding us such healthy and delicious food.

French toast not withstanding.

I picked up David from school. He seemed happy and excited. He told me about his day as I drove him home.

"And Jimmy Kenan is going to the party, too," he said. "He asked if I could spend the night at his house after the party, along with a couple other boys. You're supposed to call his mom. Or Dad can do it."

"I can do it," I said. "Do you want to spend the night?"

"Are you going to be home?" he asked.

"Um, yes," I said, "but you wouldn't be."

"That's all right," he said. "As long as you are."

"David, I wish you'd tell me why I have to be at home every night," I said. "Sometimes it cramps my style."

He shrugged. "I get nervous if you're not."

I sighed. "Well, if you want to spend the night at Jimmy's after the party, it's all right with me. And I'll be home here, too."

"Where would you go if you could spend the night some place else," he said, "without me? Rehab again?"

"No! No rehab. Sometimes when I'm at the art studio, I want to work late and if I'm tired I don't want to drive. Or like tomorrow at the Benefit, we'll be there late, and Joanie has a suite. It might be nice to stay there with her. Have a girl's night out."

He nodded. "Maybe you could try it," he said. "Tomorrow, when I'm gone. We could see how it goes."

"We'll see," I said. "Thanks for the offer."

I pulled into the driveway. Hayword's car was there. David got out of the car and ran into the house. I followed. I wondered if Hayword had read my quick and dirty *Beauty and the Zombie* treatment yet.

"Hayword?" I called as I came into the house.

"In here."

I followed David into the kitchen. Hayword sat at the table with his right leg propped up on a pillow on another chair. Eartha was cutting up something at the counter. The counter seemed to be her sweet spot.

"Thanks for taking Hayword to the doc, Eartha," I said. "That was certainly your one great thing today."

She shook her head. "You always say that before the day is over!"

I heard someone coming down the stairs.

I turned toward the sound as Fern came into the room.

She was frowning. The frown deepened when she saw me.

"Hello, baby," I said.

"Hello, Mom."

I leaned over to kiss her. She moved away. I glanced at Hayword.

"How's your ankle?" I asked Hayword.

"It's fine," Hayword said. "It's great, actually. For one thing it got me out of going to the Benefit tomorrow."

"Maybe I should fall down the stairs, too," I said. "So I can get out of it."

I didn't really want to get out of it. Not if Greg Douglas was going to be there.

"Don't they have free booze there, Mom?" Fern said. She didn't look up from her texting. "I figured you'd be all over that."

My daughter was not actually very clever. Her insults usually lacked wit.

Maybe that was why she pissed me off so much.

"I've got free booze here," I said. "No reason to leave home for that. Plus the Village Boozery delivers."

Eartha smiled as she chopped. Then she said, "There's a snack in the fridge for you, David. Some veggies and hummus. Maybe your mom wants some, too. I've already fed Fern and Hayword."

David went to the fridge and took out the plate. He brought it over to me. We sat on stools at the counter together and shared the food. He leaned up against me a little.

"What brings you to our fair village?" I asked Fern.

"It's my home, isn't it?" Fern asked. "Do I need to call and ask permission ahead of time?"

David glanced at me and rolled his eyes.

"You're welcome here any time," Hayword said. "Fern is attending a demonstration in Los Angeles tomorrow. She thought she'd come hang out with us for the evening and then we could take her into the city when we go to the Benefit. Her car wasn't working. We picked her up at the train station."

"Well," I said, as I chewed on a carrot, *"we* are not going to the benefit tomorrow. *I* am. And I'm going with Joanie. You can catch a ride with us to the hotel. You can take a cab from there."

"What are you demonstrating?" David asked. "Is that like a protest?"

"Yes," Fern said. "We're protesting the unfairness of everything. The rich keep getting richer, and the poor keep getting poorer. There's no equity in this country. Eartha, do you want to come? I bet you've been to lots of protests."

I could hear the underlying message in her words: "You've been to lots of protests, unlike my own parents who never did anything."

I smiled and ate the vegetables.

"I think I'll stick around here tomorrow," Eartha said. "But thank you for the invite."

"Eartha, you need a day off," I said. "Or days off." I realized we had never talked about any of that. We needed to pay her, too.

She shook her head. "No, I'm fine. I've been having so much fun. I want to keep doing what I've been doing, at least for a few more days."

"I don't know why they need you anyway," Fern said. "My mom doesn't do anything except sit around on her ass all day."

The kitchen got very still for a moment.

I glanced at Hayword. He looked furious, but he didn't move or say anything. David looked like he was going to cry.

Eartha put down her knife. "Don't talk so disrespectfully about your mother," she said.

"Well, at least she didn't say I sat on my *fat* ass all day," I said. "Thank you for that, daughter."

I kissed David on the top of his head. Then I picked up my purse and keys, and I walked out of my house.

I wasn't sure if I was ever coming back.

NINE

I drove around for a while. I wished I had a girlfriend I could talk to. Not that I actually wanted to talk. I could go to Joan's and get drunk.

That sounded like fun.

Christ. I hadn't even found out if Hayword liked *Beauty and the Zombie.*

David texted me right away. "Fern is a bitch."

"Don't call your sister that. Don't call any girl or woman that."

"What about boys?"

"Knock yourself out. I might not get home until after you're asleep."

"Knock yourself out."

I laughed. I texted, "Eye love u sew much."

"Sew much," he texted back.

When David was younger and learning to spell, he often got confused by the soundalikes. One year he gave me a Valentine's

Day card that read, "Eye love u sew much, Mom." So we'd been loving each other "sew much" for years.

Soon, no doubt, I wouldn't be able to tell him I loved him at all. I did dread the teen years.

Sometimes it seemed as though children got some kind of plague when they became teens. One day they were normal loving kids, and then suddenly they were monsters.

Maybe monsters was too harsh a word. And then suddenly they were zombie aliens?

Yep, that worked. Because the zombie aliens had agendas, too. Fern always had an agenda. Of course, Fern was no longer a teenager, so there went that theory.

I laughed at myself and drove to the bungalow.

I went inside the house.

It was Friday night and I was going to hide out in this house alone because my daughter was a brat?

Nope.

I pulled out my phone and stared at it.

I needed to break it off with Mark.

I knew I had to. Had to.

He was too serious.

Or maybe I was beginning to see him as part of my life.

I had to break it off.

I went to the fridge and opened it.

Mark's fixings for omelettes were still there.

I sighed. Then I texted him, "I'm at the bungalow. Could use some company. Might break all the eggs if someone doesn't stop me."

I went and sat at the kitchen table.

I got a text.

"I read the treatment." Sally. "Fucking rocks. Sequel potential. So glad I only ever fucked you and never fucked you over. Thanks, kid."

I laughed.

Another text. Hayword.

Shit. I hoped I hadn't sent him Mark's text by mistake.

"Thought the treatment was great," he wrote. "You want to start rewrites tonight?"

I didn't answer him.

I stared at the phone.

Mark wasn't answering me.

I wasn't answering Hayword.

Was this passive aggressive behavior or a pretense that we were civilized?

Another text. Hayword. "She doesn't know how she sounds."

I answered this one. "Someone should tell her." Besides Eartha. "Tell Eartha I said thanks. Be home late."

"Don't drink and drive."

Shut the fuck up.

"Shut the fuck up," I texted.

"Like daughter, like mother."

I made a noise and flung the phone across the room.

"I hate you, you motherfucker!" I screamed.

I sat on the floor and put my head in my hands. I wished I could cry. I wanted to cry. It would be a release, wouldn't it? A fucking release.

I heard a tap on my back door.

I got up and walked toward it.

Mark was standing there.

I smiled and opened the door.

"What took you so long?"

He put his arms around me, and we kissed.

Just like in the movies.

I closed the door.

"What's going on?" he asked.

I shrugged. "How'd you get here so quickly? Please tell me you aren't stalking me."

"I'm not stalking you," he said. "I told you I had a job. I finished. I changed my clothes and I was going to get an early dinner somewhere. You hungry?"

I shook my head.

I was sad. I was fucking sad.

I was mad.

I was hurt.

Shit. I was feeling all those things, and I didn't like it.

"Could you please just fuck me?" I asked.

It was that or I was going to drink myself into a stupor.

He sighed. "All right," he said, taking my hand. "But just this one time."

"Baby, fasten your seat belt," I said. "It's gonna be a long and bumpy ride."

For a few minutes, while we were making love, I felt better.

After, Mark made me an omelette. He told me what he was doing the whole time. Each step. His voice was deep and quiet. Soothing. As though he were telling me a bedtime story.

We sat on the couch together to eat the omelettes. He fed me a piece of his and I fed him pieces of mine. He started talking about farmer's markets he liked to go to, about his garden, about how he liked to dig his fingers into the ground because it felt cool and quiet and necessary. Tears began to stream down my face. I didn't notice them at first. Then Mark wiped them away with the palm of his hand. Then he kissed them. We went to bed and I curled into a ball. He curled up around me. Was I the seashell and he the ocean? Or was I the empty air that sounded like the ocean and he was the shell?

I didn't like either of those images.

I waited until Mark fell to sleep. Then I slowly extricated myself from his arms. I went to the kitchen and found a bottle of wine. I sat down on the couch and drank it.

I awakened to the sound of someone pounding on the front door. At first I couldn't tell what it was. The room spun a bit when I sat up. It was dark.

"Brooke! I know you're in there!"

Oh fuck. Hayword.

Well, I supposed he was bound to turn up eventually.

I got up from the couch and staggered to the door.

"Go away!" I shouted.

"Brooke, David is hysterical."

"I told him I'd be home," I said.

"Open the fucking door," Hayword said. "It's three a.m. Someone's gonna call the police."

I opened the door but left the light off.

He limped over the threshold. I didn't move. I didn't want him coming any further into the house.

"I'll come home now," I said. "I thought your ankle was too hurt to dance. But you can drive down the hill?"

"Eartha drove me," he said. "I had to go and wake her up."

"Thank god you didn't bring Fern."

Oh shit. I had said that out loud.

"I didn't want her to see this."

"See what?" I said. "It's a fucking house."

I was still drunk.

"Brooke," he said. "You've got to stop doing this. Stop punishing yourself and me. Alberto didn't die because of anything you did or anything I did or didn't do."

"But did you ever wonder," I said, "what would have happened if he'd never been born? If all of that had never happened? I mean, then maybe everything wouldn't have fallen apart. Sometimes I feel so stupid. I was so gullible."

Hayword tried to put his arms around me. I pushed him away.

"Come home with us now," he said. "We'll get your car in the morning."

"David's a good boy," I said. "A good boy. Alberto was too. But maybe . . . Fern is not a nice person. I think there must have been a mix-up at the hospital."

Hayword laughed. He had always found me amusing, too, just like Mark.

"Come home," he said.

I shook my head. Then I nodded. "I will."

"You can't drive," he said. "Have whoever is with you drive you home. But David's pretty bad off. Have some coffee and a shower. Then come home."

"Okay," I said. "Okay. Now go away. You're invading my space, man." I giggled. "My spaceman."

I pushed Hayword out of the house. He limped down the walk.

I shut the door.

Fuck. Fuck. Fuck.

I turned around. I could see Mark's outline inside the dark bedroom.

"Did you hear all that?" I asked.

"Yep," he said. "I'll make you coffee."

"I'll shower," I said.

First I threw up.

I had been doing too much of that lately.

How come suddenly I couldn't hold my liquor?

Wine wasn't liquor. It was fermented fruit. Of course it was going to make me sick.

I took a shower.

I felt better. Mark gave me a cup of coffee when I came out of the bathroom. He sat on the edge of the bed next to me.

"Brooke, in the last two days, you've gotten drunk twice and passed out at least once. That's a lot of brain cells you're killing.

You asked me if my alkie-dar was on. Well, it wasn't. Now it is. I've known you for nearly a year and I've never seen you drunk before today."

"That you know of," I said.

"That I know of," he said. He reached for my hand and held it between both of his. He glanced away for a moment, and then he looked directly at me. "I can't be around you if you're drinking like this. It's not good for my sobriety. It's not good for you."

"Are you leaving me?" I asked.

"I'll take you home," he said. "I'll drive you to rehab. I'll take you to a therapist. I'll sit with you when you want a drink. I'll go with you to AA meetings. But I can't be with you when you're drinking."

I pulled my hand away from him.

"I've been to rehab," I said. "I've talked to a therapist. I can go without a drink. That's not the problem."

"Whatever's eating you isn't getting better," he said. "You might want to face it, whatever it is."

I wasn't going to argue with him. Or defend myself.

"I love you, Brooke," he said.

"I don't love you," I said quickly. "This is me. This is the real fucking me. Love me or leave me. Oh wait. You've decided. You're going to leave me."

He rubbed his face. I could see dampness on his fingers.

I stood. "Well, good," I said. "I was going to end it anyway. I met someone. Someone who understands me. You and I are at the end of our run."

Mark stood. "Don't say anything that you'll be sorry for later."

I looked down at him.

Please don't leave me.

"Already said and done," I said.

We left the house together, walked down the block to Mark's

truck. He drove me to my house. We sat together in the truck for a minute.

"Do I smell like I've been drinking?" I asked. "I don't want David to know."

Mark didn't say anything.

"It's better this way," I said. I didn't want to get out of the truck. "If you really knew me, you'd be sorry. I mean, you'd probably stay for a while, but then you'd go."

"What more could I possibly know about you?" he said. "I know you've been cheating on your husband for what, eight years? My wife cheated on me. Thought it ruined my life. But then I try to take you away from your family. I don't think very highly of myself, but I do admire you. I've always known you're more than some lonely woman I fucked."

"I'm not lonely," I said. "And it's been eleven years."

"What do you mean?" he said. "You told me you got the house eight years ago. And Alberto died ten years ago. That's when you caught Hayword with another woman."

I felt completely sober. And completely unable to get out of the truck.

"He died almost ten years ago," I said. "I met this man. He worked with Hayword on a picture. He was nice. He paid attention to me. I wasn't just the wife, I was somebody. I had just had a baby so I felt frumpy and ugly, like some kind of breeding cow. And he was beautiful. Ryan Nichols. I was so in love with him. I was like a teenager. Like when I first was in love with Hayword. I had never cheated on Hayword before. But I was unhappy. This deep unhappiness. I thought Hayword was living this beautiful life and I was nothing. I was invisible. When Ryan and I had sex, it was like I was alive again. I was fucking besotted. I wanted to leave my family. I think I would have. Then I got pregnant, and Ryan was gone. Just disappeared. Changed his phone number. It was awful. I thought I would die."

I stared at my house.

"Hayword took care of me," I said. "He forgave me. Even that made me angry. Why should he forgive me? Because I'd been happy for a brief moment in time? I hurt all the time. I wanted to forget what had happened. But I had this baby. He was so beautiful. He reminded me of Ryan. Something about his eyes."

I breathed deeply. "And then he died. Everyone thought I was so unhappy because he died. And I was. I loved him. But I had been unhappy before. I was unhappy during his life. Then I was unhappy after. I didn't really change, Mark. I was still the same unhappy person. I wasn't more unhappy. I wasn't less un-happy. Isn't that the definition of a sociopath?"

The door to the house opened. Hayword stood on the top step looking out.

"Then I found Hayword with someone else," I said, "after he had promised to make everything better, right after we buried Alberto and I knew then that he had never loved Alberto like he loved the other kids, like he promised me he would. And now I could blame him. Blame him for everything. I told everyone he had cheated on me. He never told anyone that I had cheated on him. Never told anyone that Alberto was not his son. He waits. Waits for me to get better. For it to be the same as it was before Alberto died. But the thing is, Mark—" I turned to look at him. "—the thing is that everything is the same as before Alberto died."

"Brooke," Mark said.

I turned away, opened the truck door, and got out. I went up the walk. Hayword held out his hand for me. I slipped my hand into his, and we went back into the house.

David was asleep when I went into his room. I lay down on the bed next to him. I watched him sleep and breathe, sleep and breathe. He opened his eyes once and whispered, "Momma."

Then he went back to sleep. But for those few moments he had his eyes open, he looked just like his brother.

TEN

I woke up in David's bed. He was up and gone. I could hear him downstairs somewhere, laughing and talking with his father.

I got up and went into our room.

I felt strangely refreshed. I could hear the wind blowing outside, could see the trees rocking in the wind. To the southeast, the sky looked a little smoky or ruddy.

I didn't hear Eartha or Fern.

Maybe Eartha had adopted Fern. That would certainly be her one great thing for today as far as I was concerned.

I laughed, grabbed my phone, and lay back on the bed. I was feeling downright . . . okay.

I checked my messages. I was to pick up Joan no later than five. Unless we wanted to go earlier and drink our lunch somewhere.

No.

A text from Mark. "I'll see you on Monday as planned. We'll talk. Call any time."

"Thanks." I texted. "Lv."

He knew the truth, and he still wanted me. I didn't understand it. Hayword was the same way.

Did I surround myself with men with incredibly bad taste and poor judgment?

I went downstairs to the TV room. We were supposed to call this room something else. When we bought the house, the real estate agents had some name for it, but that's where we put the TV and that's where we watched it. So it was the TV room. Hayword had his foot up on a stool. David sat next to him. They were watching a hockey game.

I went over to the couch and kissed the top of Hayword's head. Then I went and sat next to David.

"Good morning, you two," I said.

"Mom, it's way past noon," David said. "This would be the afternoon."

"Good *afternoon,* you two," I said.

"Quite the slackard today," Hayword said.

"I know," I said. "David, I'm sorry I scared you last night. I went to the art studio and I stayed too late. I got tired and fell to sleep on the couch."

"Fern said you were drunk," David said.

I glanced at Hayword.

"Your sister is actually right," I said. "For once. Where is she anyway?"

"Eartha took her into town for her demonstration," Hayword said. "They're going to make a day of it. Protesting and shopping. The best of both worlds, I guess."

"Wow, that woman does more great things in a day than I do in a year," I said. "We should give her a raise. Anyway, David, I did drink too much. I'm going to stop that."

"You're going to stop drinking?" David asked. He seemed overly pleased by this prospect.

"I'm going to stop drinking to excess," I said.

"Can't you stop altogether?" David asked. "It makes me nervous."

Oh fuck. What kind of mother was I if I couldn't say yes to that.

"Okay, David," I said. "I won't promise you that I'll never drink, but I won't drink today. How's that?"

"But tonight's the Benefit," Hayword said.

David looked at me.

"I don't have to drink at the Benefit," I said. "Please. It'll be a good time without a drop to drink." I smiled. Hayword looked skeptical. "Okay. I've got to get ready. You have a good day."

"Are you coming home tonight?" David asked.

"Do I have your permission to run away from home?" I asked.

He shook his head.

"Okay, then. I guess I'll be home tonight," I said.

Joan and I decided to leave early for the Benefit. I carried my specially made low-cut red dress to the car, and then I drove across the street to Joan's house. It was the first time I had seen Bernie since the bathtub incident, and he wouldn't look me in the eyes.

When I mentioned this to Joan once we were in my car, she said, "I've gotten a couple really good fucks out of it. I think he's imagining you and me in bed together. We should get naked together and take pictures, so I can show them to him and that'll get him really hard."

The road out of the village and onto the freeway was blocked by fire trucks. Smoke billowed from trees in the distance, but I didn't see any flames.

"We could run the fire line," Joan said. "I bet we could make it."

"No, we couldn't," I said. "You just want to be rescued by some cute fire fighter."

"Yes, take me to your leader," she said.

We left the village in a roundabout way. People and cars kept coming out of and going into the smoke. I tried to find a way around it all.

We ended up far out of our way, on the 401, headed to the city. We soon left the smoke behind as we tooled down the expressway. Hardly anyone was on the freeway. The sun was out. Palm trees moved slightly with the wind, as though they were hula dancers. We put the windows down and turned up the radio.

"Ventura highway, baby!" I said.

Joan and I laughed and sang off key to whatever rock 'n' roll song was on the radio.

I couldn't remember the last time I had felt this good.

Maybe the truth did set us free.

I looked at Joan and she was smiling, too.

It was a glorious moment in time.

Ahead I could see traffic.

We put our windows up again.

"Joanie, I'm fucking the plumber," I said, apropos of nothing.

"What? You mean the guy who saw me—who saw me naked in the bathtub?" she asked.

"Yep."

"Oh, I'm mortified," she said.

"Why? He doesn't care," I said. "He's a nice guy."

"Are you going to leave Hayword?" she asked.

"For Mark?" I said. "No. I've had lovers on the side for years. I don't leave Hayword."

"Why not?"

I laughed. "What do you mean why not? He's my husband.

He's the father of my children." At least some of them. "He's a good man, kind, good-looking, works hard."

"But you hate him," she said.

We caught up to traffic.

"I don't hate him," I said. "What makes you think that?"

"Brooke, you hate everyone."

"What? I do not," I said. "I don't hate you. I don't hate David. What are you talking about?"

"Hey, don't shoot the messenger," she said. "I thought you hated Hayword. I've never seen you be nice to him. Or anyone else for that matter."

"Aren't I nice to you?"

She shrugged.

"Nice is overrated," I said.

"Yeah, but sometimes it's . . . nice," she said. "You are quick with the quips. Sometimes people deserve them. But sometimes they don't. Like yesterday you told the three of us that we reminded you of the balls on a ball-less terrier."

"That doesn't make any sense," I said.

"Still, it was insulting," she said.

"Essentially I was saying that you reminded me of something that doesn't exist," I said.

"Exactly," she said. "No one likes to be told they're nothing."

"Okay, noted," I said. "I'll try not to be such an asshole."

"An asshole on a shitless terrier," she said.

"That would mean I was completely useless," I said.

"Now you're getting it," she said.

I looked over at her. "You're smarter than I give you credit for."

"See," she said. "Was that a compliment or an insult?"

"Uh, neither. Just a statement of . . . my opinion."

"Oh, take this exit," she said. "There's a guy at that gas station on the corner who is too beautiful for words."

I laughed. Then I drove us off the freeway.

We got a suite at the Shilton Hotel. We had them bring up lunch. Joan got champagne and some kind of mixed drink. I asked for coffee and water. Joan didn't ask me why I wasn't drinking. Maybe after Thursday she figured it was a good idea.

After lunch, we took turns taking a shower, and then we helped each other get dressed, put on our makeup, and do our hair.

"Do you love him, this plumber?" she asked.

"His name is Mark," I said. "You know that. Do I love him? I don't even know what that means. I've been seeing him for nearly a year. I have a lot of affection for him."

"A year?" Joan said. "That's more than a fuck. That's an affair. That's longer than one of my marriages."

"Really?"

Joan laughed. "No! I've only been married twice. I divorced the first guy after five years."

"Did you feel like you were a failure," I said, "because you divorced? I mean, did you feel like you had wasted those five years?"

"No! We were happy together," she said. "And then we weren't. So we divorced."

"You're not happy with Bernie," I said. "Why don't you divorce?"

"I don't know," she said. "Same reasons you gave. I love him. He's the father of my kids, worthless bastards that they are. He's got money, and I don't have to work too hard. It's easier to stay with him. Divorce is not easy or fun even when it's amicable."

"Can you imagine if we said these kinds of things to our younger selves?" I said. "What would they say? 'You stayed with someone because it was easier? What about passion? What about happiness?'"

Joan made a noise. "I think if my younger self knew how her older self was going to turn out, she would have blown her brains out."

"Good thing she didn't know then," I said.

Finally it was time to go down to the Benefit. We weren't walking the red carpet. We didn't have to greet anyone at the door. We had no responsibilities tonight except to have a good time.

Joan and I rode the elevator together, both of us dressed in red dresses, our arms linked. The doors opened, and we stepped off the elevator and walked to the ballroom. We stood on the threshold and looked inside. The room was dimly lit but bright enough for us to see all the sparkling jewels and tanned bosoms. Men in black and women in red, blue, purple, cream, yellow. Bernie turned and saw us. He smiled. He looked smitten. I looked at Joan. She was smiling, too.

"See you later, love," she said.

The two of them went off together.

I walked around, talking to people I knew, introducing myself to people I didn't know. Sally St. James was there with her husband. He was a good looking man. He didn't smile much, except when Sally said something. He, too, seemed clearly in love.

And then this gorgeous white-haired man walked into the ballroom. He stood so straight and tall, as though he was a Marine dressed in a tuxedo.

"Wow." I had almost forgotten about him, but now here he was: Greg Douglas.

Greg saw me, smiled, and walked over to me.

We quickly embraced.

Man, he smelled good.

"I'm so glad you came," I said.

"Wouldn't have missed it," he said. "Would you care to dance?"

"I'd love to," I said.

We danced through several songs. I introduced him as a friend of Hayword's and mine whenever someone stopped to say hello. Then we sat at a table away from the others and talked. We didn't sit close together. I was a married woman. I had to be discreet.

We got up and danced to the next slow dance. He held me close. I could feel his hard-on. I looked at him.

I guessed this meant he liked me, he really liked me.

"I feel like I've been waiting for you for years," I whispered.

He pushed himself up against me. "I've always been attracted to you," he said. "But I couldn't do anything about it. Now we meet again like this, at this difficult time in your life. I think it's a sign."

Yes, a sign. That was it.

Maybe it was meant to be.

Not that I believed in any of that shit.

"I want to feel your cunt around my cock," he said.

He whispered it, but I glanced around. Had anyone else heard?

I would not have guessed that Greg Douglas was a dirty talker.

That was all right.

A little dirty talk never hurt.

And my cunt responded appropriately.

"I want to feel your creamy cunt around my cock," he said.

It ain't that creamy any more, I thought. I ain't no spring chicken.

I wanted to laugh.

And I wanted to take off my clothes and do the wild thing with him.

"I won't ever hurt you," he said. "You must know that I'll always protect you. You will come so hard. I promise you. I've never wanted anyone so much. I wanted to fuck you the other day. Wanted my cock in your cunt. Would have happened, too, if it wasn't for that earthquake. Mother Nature responding to our passion. Never wanted anyone the way I want you."

Someone was bound to hear. We had to get away.

And even though his dirty talk sounded silly, I was very wet. I was ready to be fucked and fucked hard, as he said.

"Meet me in room 405," I said. I slipped the keycard in his pocket. "I'll be up in five minutes."

The song ended. I thanked him, and we walked away from each other. I found someone I knew and didn't care about—pretty much everyone there—and I had a quick chat.

Then I went to the bathroom. I went into a stall and closed the door. Oh my god. My vagina was pulsating. I was going to come before I got upstairs to Greg. Maybe I should masturbate before I went up to the suite, so I wouldn't come too soon. So it would last longer.

No. I wasn't having sex in a hotel bathroom, even if it was only with myself.

I would have sex upstairs in a hotel room with an almost complete stranger.

At least I hadn't had anything to drink.

I got in the elevator and went up to the fourth floor. When I got to 405, I realized I had given my keycard to Greg, so I wouldn't be able to get in.

I knocked softly. The door opened, but I didn't see anyone.

I went inside. The door closed behind me.

Greg was right there. He pressed me up against the wall.

"Do you want it?" he asked.

We kissed. He pushed himself up against me, and he began dry humping me against the wall. It was working. I was about to come. Then he pulled up my dress and put his finger between my panties and my skin. His fingers found the wet place and slid up easily inside. He finger fucked me until I almost came, was about to come, *please don't stop, please don't stop, please don't stop,* and then he pulled his fingers out. He began kissing me again and leading me into the bedroom. He quickly took off his clothes. I could see his erect penis. Knew it would be inside me any second and then I would come. Then I would have an orgasm that would rock my world. *Now, now, now.*

"Take off your clothes," he said.

I got quickly naked.

His penis was pulsing.

My vagina was pulsing.

Now we had to put the two together.

"Get on the floor on the your hands and knees," he said.

"What?"

"On the floor on your hands and knees," he said. "You want it, don't you? You want my hard cock up inside your cunt. Now get on your hands and knees like the little bitch you are."

"Pardon me?" I said.

"Don't you want it?" he said. "Don't you want to be punished for all the wrong you've done?"

I suddenly felt very naked.

But I was also still aroused.

For an instant—only an instant—I considered it. Maybe I did need some humiliation to get my mind right.

Fuck. That. Shit.

"This is the way I like it," he said, in a stage whisper. "Don't you? I thought we were on the same page here."

"I'm not a Catholic," I said. "I'm not really carrying around any deep-seated guilt about anything I've done."

"Really?" His voice was no longer seductive. Just perplexed. "After all the secrets you told me the other day."

"I don't remember telling you any secrets," I said.

"When I put you to bed," he said, "you told me all about your secret affairs, about your baby not being your husband's son. You said you felt like you should be punished. I knew then we were simpatico."

His erection was beginning to fall.

Mine certainly was.

"No!" I said. I grabbed the sheet and covered myself up. "I'll have sex with you but not like a dog. I don't need to be punished or humiliated."

His erection was completely gone. I couldn't even tell he had a penis or balls.

"Are you telling me you can't do it unless . . . ?"

"'fraid so, darlin'," he said.

Don't call me darlin'.

He picked up his tighty whities and put them on. Then his T-shirt, his shirt, pants, cummerbund, his slacks. He sat on the bed and pulled on his socks and shoes.

He looked at me. "Different strokes for different folks," he said. "I'll see you in the funny papers."

He tossed the keycard on the bed.

And then he left.

As soon as the door closed behind him, I started to laugh.

"Oh my god," I said. I shuddered. I couldn't believe his fingers had touched me. "Bleck!"

I didn't know if I ever wanted to have sex again.

I wanted to call Mark and tell him all about it.

Or maybe Hayword.

No! Sheesh.

Joan.

I would go tell Joan. She would laugh her ass off.

I got dressed again and went downstairs. I found Joan and pulled herself aside and told her what had happened. She laughed so hard she nearly pissed her pants. She laughed so loudly that half the people in the ballroom looked over at us. Bernie came over to see if she was all right.

Just about then I got a phone call from Eartha.

I went outside to talk to her.

"Everything all right?" I asked.

Outside the winds were strong and hot. It felt hot even though it was evening in January.

I went back into the hotel and sat at a table in the lobby.

"Fern is in jail," Eartha said. "And I don't have any money to bail her out. She told me not to call you, but she'll have to stay the night if someone doesn't come. She doesn't have any money either. They put her away from the other protestors because they got full. She's with the derelicts. At least that's what she said."

"I'll be right there," I said. "Which precinct? Do you have the address?"

I went back to the Benefit and told Joan that I had to leave. Then I had the parking valet get my car. As I slid into the seat, I realized I should have gone upstairs and taken off the dress and put on my jeans. Ah well. Fern would have to deal with it. I put the address into the GPS, and then I followed directions to the police station.

I felt a little silly walking from the parking lot to the police station in my evening gown. It was a busy Saturday night at the cop shop. Of course I'd never been at a police station on a Saturday night, so maybe it was slower than usual. What did I know? Despite the activity, it was quieter than I would have thought. In all the movies and TV shows, every cop shop was noisy.

I got a couple of wolf whistles. Wasn't sure who did the whistling, but Eartha saw me and came over.

"Sorry, Brooke," she said. "I don't know what happened. We

got separated and then suddenly the police were pepper spraying and arresting people."

"It's not your fault, I'm sure," I said. "Where do I pay?"

She took me to the window where I paid Fern's bail money. Fern had already been arraigned with a group of other protestors. Eartha and I sat on a wooden bench and waited for her.

Finally the door buzzed open and Fern came out to us. She looked a little pale.

"Do you need to wash up or anything?" I asked.

"Mom, what are you doing here?" she said. "You look like the whore of Babylon."

"This whore of Babylon can leave you here," I said, "or I can give you a ride home. Your choice."

Fern walked ahead of us. Eartha put her arm through mine as we followed.

"You want her?" I asked. "Cuz you can have her. She's yours."

We got into the car, with Fern sitting in the back. I drove us away from the police station and headed in the direction of home. I glanced back at my daughter every once in a while. She looked like she was going to be sick.

"Do you want me to pull over?" I asked. "Or take you to the hospital? Were you pepper sprayed?"

"Yes," she said. "I was standing up for what is right while you fat cats sat around eating caviar on crackers and drinking champagne."

"There was caviar?" I asked. "Damn it. I missed it. We can go back and get some."

"Did you have a good day?" I asked Eartha.

"Yes, we had fun," she said. "Some really good people out there."

"Maybe next time I'll join you," I said. "I'm proud of you for standing up for what you believe in, Fern."

"Don't be sarcastic," she said. "I don't feel very well."

"I'm not being sarcastic," I said. "I meant it."

"Oh. I don't know if we'll do any good."

"How's school?"

"I don't want to talk, Mom. My stomach is upset."

We traveled the rest of the way in near silence. At least Fern wasn't screaming at me. So a little pepper spray slapped the bite out of her. I should remember that and stock up.

Bad mother.

I smiled.

"Sorry about last night," I told Eartha. "Those days are over. I'm on the straight and narrow."

I frowned: I didn't really want to be on the straight and narrow.

"How about on the windy and the broad," Eartha said. She must have noticed my frown. "You could come up with something. You're the writer."

"I wrote up a treatment for the zombie movie," I said.

"Hayword told me," she said. "He was very happy. Did you have fun?"

I shrugged. "It was all right."

We got off the expressway, but we weren't able to go very far. Fire trucks blocked the way. I turned the car and took us a back way, up and around and down again.

"Mom, these roads are making me sick," she said. "Stop the car, stop the car!"

I stopped the car. Fern got out. I heard her throwing up. I got out and went over to her.

"You want me to hold your hair?"

"I'm done," she said. "I don't want to go on that windy road home. It's making me feel worse."

"Okay," I said.

I drove us to the bungalow.

I parked the car in the driveway.

Eartha didn't say anything. She knew where we were.

Fern didn't say anything either. She trudged to the front door, got the extra key from under the rock, and went inside. I followed. She went straight into the bathroom and threw up.

I got her water.

She came out of the bathroom and stumbled to the couch.

"How did you know where that key was?" I asked.

"Come on, Mom," she said. "Anyone could figure it out. I come here sometimes on the weekends, and during that month you were gone. Or the almost month. It's been my home away from home."

"I never saw any sign of you," I said.

"I'm good at being invisible," she said. She looked at Eartha. "This is where Mom brings all her boyfriends. Slut Central."

"Fern," Eartha said. "I thought you wanted to talk to your mother. Remember what we talked about. About you being kind and respectful."

I got a cloth from the bathroom. I ran cool water over it. Then I squeezed it and brought it back to the living room and put it across Fern's forehead. She let me be near her. She closed her eyes.

"It's my fault," Fern said.

"What's your fault?" I asked.

"When we were kids, I told David that Alberto died because you weren't home. Little boys died when their mothers went away, I said. I was mad at him about something. It was a mean thing to say. I tried to take it back, but he believed it."

"But I was home when Alberto died," I said. "That doesn't make any sense."

Fern opened her eyes. She sat up a little so that she wasn't close to me. I got up and sat in one of the chairs. Eartha sat in another one.

"I've asked him why he gets so scared," I said. "He doesn't remember. I'm sure he doesn't remember you telling him that."

"If you're so sure then it must be true," Fern said.

I shook my head.

"What did I ever do to you that makes you hate me so much?" I asked. "I birthed you. I took care of you. I took you to every dance class, music lesson, doctor's appointment. I was always there for you and with you, and you always hated me."

"I didn't hate you," Fern said. "And you weren't always there. You were never there. Maybe when I was very young. But then you were gone! It made me so angry. I wanted you to come back. You were so sad all that time. And it got worse after Alberto died."

She started to cry.

"Everything got worse after that," she said. "And that was my fault. I must have done something wrong. I must have fed him something wrong. Or put him to bed wrong. He was a perfectly healthy boy and then he was dead!"

"We've told you again and again that you didn't do anything wrong," I said. "He just died. No one was to blame."

"David thinks he's to blame," Fern said. "He thinks Alberto died because he—David—cried too much. You and Dad always talk about how much David cried those first two years, so he's convinced he cried Alberto to death."

I laughed.

It wasn't funny, but the laugh just came out.

Fern wiped her tears.

"It's not funny," Fern said.

"I know it's not," I said.

She started to sob.

"What is wrong, Fern?"

"There's more, Mom," she said. "You have no idea what I've done."

Besides treat me like shit all of your life. You mean there's more?

"I burned down the house," she said.

"What?"

I felt instantly sick to my stomach. It couldn't be true.

"You did not burn down the house," I said.

"I did." She was crying so hard that she could barely breathe. She started hiccupping as she tried to catch her breath. I went and sat next to her. She moved away.

"I was so tired of you being sad," she said. "Dad was all right. He moved on. He made certain we were okay. You just sat in Alberto's room. You cried and cried. It was worse when you didn't cry. And you and Dad didn't even seem to like each other. I thought if we had to move, if we left Alberto's stuff behind, we could leave it all behind. I thought we could be happy again. So I waited until everyone was gone and I started the fire."

"They said it was an electrical fire," I said. "You couldn't have done this. You weren't even thirteen years old."

"I did it!" she screamed. "I put a lit match near the dryer and I left it there and the house burned. I did it, I did it! And nothing got better. Nothing. We all kind of disappeared. And sometimes I wish so much that Alberto was never born because then he wouldn't have died!" She was yelling. I reached for her. She tried to pull away from me, but I wouldn't let her. I put my arms around her and held her as she sobbed.

"I've thought the same things," I said. "It's normal and natural." Although I hadn't realized it until that moment. "Only Alberto didn't cause it, not his birth or death. I was sad. I was sad before he was born. I was unhappy with my life. He wasn't to blame and you aren't to blame. Well, maybe you're to blame for burning down the house; I don't really know about that."

She laughed a little. "Why couldn't you be happy?"

"I don't know," I said. "Somehow I got off track. I followed your father. Not that I'm blaming him. I followed him when I didn't want to. I settled for things I didn't want. And then I began to disappear. I don't know."

"I've been worried for ten years that someone is going to find out," Fern said. "And they'll send me to jail and they'll make you give the insurance money back because they'll figure it was an inside job."

I looked at her. "I don't think that's going to happen," I said. "In fact, it's not possible. They've built another house on top of our old one. They couldn't reconstruct anything. Besides, no one has doubted the findings. You're safe. You're in the clear. I'm not glad you burned the house down, but I was glad to leave it." I let her go and looked at her. "Have you burned down any other houses?"

"No!"

"You didn't go into psychology because you're an arsonist or anything? I mean, there are a lot of fires out there right now."

"No, Mom, no!"

Fern sighed, shuddering a little as she breathed out.

"Why did you come here when I wasn't here?" I asked.

Fern looked around. "I wanted to be closer to you," she said.

"But I wasn't here," I said.

She nodded. "I know."

ELEVEN

Fern slept in the guest bedroom. The guest bedroom that had never been used before. I got a blanket and pillow for Eartha to sleep on the couch. I called Hayword and told him where we were. We decided we wouldn't tell David, since he had a sleepover. If he called me in the middle of the night and asked where I was, I would decide then what to tell him.

I took a long hot shower. I wanted a drink, I gotta tell ya, but I knew there wasn't anything in the house. I had downed what was left the night before.

I crawled under the covers and thought about my day. Greg Douglas turned out to be a pervert. Who would have thought? Although I suppose pervert was too strong a word. If consensual adults wanted to humiliate one another—or pretend to—who was I to object? My own daughter called my little home Slut Central.

Perhaps beauty was not the only thing in the eye of the beholder.

I could still see Greg Douglas standing in front of me naked, strong and proud as his erection withered.

So glad I had not laughed out loud.

I closed my eyes and fell to sleep.

I dreamed I was at a zombie ball and we were all dressed to the nines.

I heard someone whispering my name.

I opened my eyes.

It was still dark out.

I saw a shadow next to my bed.

"Brooke." Eartha's voice.

"What's wrong?" I quickly sat up.

"I have to talk to you about something."

"Now? What time is it? Is Fern all right?"

"It's something after six, I think," she said. "Fern is fine. I checked on her."

"Can't this wait until morning?" I asked.

"It is morning."

"I mean real morning," I said. "Your one great thing today would be to let me sleep."

"It's important," she said. "I made coffee."

"All right." I got out of bed. Felt chilly, so I found a pair of slacks and a shirt and pulled them on. Then I went into the living room. Fern's door was closed. The house creaked a bit from the winds. One dim light was on in the corner of the living room. I sat in one of the chairs. Eartha brought me a cup of coffee. I held it in my hands to warm up. She sat on the couch across from me. She had already folded up the blanket and put it on the pillow at the end of the couch.

I felt strangely awake.

"I have to tell you something," Eartha said.

"Never a good way to start a conversation," I said. I took

a sip of coffee. Damn. This woman could do almost anything. This was a great cup of coffee. How had she done it? I didn't even think I had coffee in the house, besides instant, and this was not instant coffee.

Eartha cleared her throat. "I want you to know that I have really enjoyed spending time with you and your family. It has been amazing. One of the most amazing weeks of my life, actually."

I didn't know what to say. This had been the week everything had fallen apart. Or so it seemed to me.

"I'm glad you enjoyed yourself," I said.

And?

"I've been here under false pretenses," she said. "I should have been honest with you from the start. I want you to know that everything was done with the absolute best intentions for you."

"What the fuck are you talking about?" I asked.

"I'm an interventionist," she said. "I often work with VIPs and famous people who don't want to go to rehab or a clinic."

I stared at her.

"What?"

"Hayword called me," she said. "He had gotten my name from a friend of a friend of his. I can't reveal that person's name, of course. He said you'd been to rehab and it hadn't worked, but you wouldn't get help, and he was afraid something bad was going to happen."

"What?"

"I said I'd be glad to come and talk with you," she said. "He thought you'd never agree to it. He begged me to come stay with the family for a few days and see if he was overreacting or not. I said I couldn't deceive you. But I let myself be convinced it was for your own good. I loved *Love and Other Insanities*. It was so big-hearted and beautiful and funny. I couldn't let the person who wrote that disappear into addiction. Or so I told myself. I was wrong. I should have been straight with you all along."

I wanted to say "what" again, but I realized that was getting repetitious.

Plus, what she was telling me was beginning to sink in.

"So you're saying you coming to the house was a complete set up?" I said. "You weren't some homeless gal wandering the streets?"

"I have done some wandering," Eartha said, "and most everything I ever told you was the absolute truth."

"Hayword told you all about our lives?" I said.

"He did," she said. "About the affairs, the baby, his death, the art studio."

I didn't know what to say.

I was actually speechless.

"I thought we were becoming friends," I said. "I was beginning to trust you."

"I know," she said. "I felt that, too. So I had to tell you."

I took a sip of coffee.

I wondered if I should hurl the coffee at her.

Or beat the shit out of her.

Or should I ask her questions?

I got up and went into the bedroom and got my phone. I called Hayword.

"Hello?"

Sounded like I woke him up.

Good.

"Get your ass down here," I said. "I know who Eartha is. I'm holding her hostage until you get here."

He coughed. "All right," he said. "I'll be there soon."

I went back into the living room and sat down.

"I guess this explains why Joan saw Violeta in Los Angeles," I said. "Violeta never left home."

"She didn't want to do it," Eartha said.

"But it's difficult to turn down a paid vacation," I said. "How about you? Why did you agree to the deception? Did Hayword offer you lots of money?"

Eartha shook her head. "I'm getting paid my standard fee."

"So if you had been honest with me," I said, "how would this have worked?"

"I would have come in and talked to you," she said, "and then we would have worked the program together. I would have taken you to private AA meetings. Things like that."

"And you think I need all that?" I asked.

"What do you think?"

Now that made me want to scream.

I kept my voice down.

I didn't want to wake Fern.

"Tell me what *you* think," I said. "My husband obviously thinks I'm a raging drunk. What's your opinion?"

"I think anyone who drinks to near blackout two days in a row has a problem."

"Who knows about this?" I asked. "Do the kids? The women in the Enclave?"

"As far as I know, only Hayword and me."

"All this time I wasn't the only one with a dirty little secret," I said. "You were so good at so many different things. How'd you do that? I was completely fooled by you. Completely."

"I can do lots of different things," Eartha said. "I wasn't trying to fool you. I was trying to be with you to figure out how I can help you."

"Can you bring my son back? No. Can you prevent me from having an affair eleven years ago? No. Can you tell me how my life got so off track? No. And who gives a fuck how? I'm here. I know I'm more fortunate than 99 percent of the world, even with a dead child, and I feel—"

What? What did I feel?

I sat there for a moment.

Maybe it was for many moments.

What did I feel? What did I feel?

"I feel so goddamn angry," I said. "And if I'm not angry, I'm sad. I much prefer the anger." I sighed. "Is Eartha even your real name?"

"Does it matter?"

"That means it isn't your real name," I said.

Suddenly the door opened and Hayword and David walked in. Hayword was no longer limping, and David looked sleepy.

"When I left I noticed smoke from the fire," Hayword said, "so I went and got David. I feel better if he's with us."

I nodded. David came over to me, and I hugged him.

The door to Fern's room opened. She came out, rubbing her eyes. For a moment, I could see the little girl she had once been.

I smiled. Couldn't help myself. There had been a time when she wasn't spitting venom at me, even though it was difficult to remember.

"Eartha, could you take the kids to the donut shop?" I said. "It's only a few blocks down." I got my keys and tossed them to her. "Hayword and I need to talk."

I thought Fern might offer up resistance. She didn't.

"There's some clean clothes in my closet you can wear," I said. "If you don't want to put on yours."

"Dad said you were in jail yesterday," David said. "Was that fun? Did anyone try to kill you?"

"Yeah," Fern said, "the cops."

A few minutes later, Eartha, Fern, and David left the house. It wasn't quite night any longer. Black was turning gray.

"How could you bring Eartha into our home like that?" I asked. "I thought part of recovery was being completely honest."

"You're supposed to be honest," he said. "I'm not in recovery. I was trying to save my wife. My life."

We both stood in the living room, several feet away from one another.

"But why now?" I asked. "What's changed? Haven't we been living like this for years?"

"I've been waiting," he said. "I've been patient. I thought you needed time to grieve. But it hasn't gotten any better. The drinking was worse. And you'd been seeing this new guy for almost a year. I felt like I should do something."

I laughed. "So because I was fucking the same guy for almost a year, you thought I needed help? Or did you think I was going to run off with him?"

"Both," he said. He sat on the couch, leaned forward, and ran his fingers through his hair. "I want our life back, Brooke. I'm sorry I had sex with that woman. I'm so, so sorry. If I could take it back, I would. But it's done and over with. There's nothing I can do about it. I want our life back!"

I sat across from him. "What life do you want back?"

"The one we had before Alberto died," he said.

"But I wasn't happy in that life either," I said. "I hadn't been happy for a long time."

"Why? We were successful," he said. "You had the family you always wanted. We were living this dream."

"This was never my dream," I said. "I wanted *us*. I wanted us and our kids. I wanted us to work together. I liked that. I didn't like the way you were here. I'm not trying to blame you."

"That's new," he said.

He was right. That was new.

I didn't want to blame him any more.

"You love it here," I said. "You love your work. I think that's great. I don't love it here. I don't like the weather. I don't like the people I meet. I don't like the company I keep. I don't like who I am here. We wanted to write great plays. We wanted to do great work. Now you're writing zombie pictures."

"So what?" he said. "We're entertainers, Brooke. That's what we've always been. You always thought we should do something different. I didn't. I wanted to write stories, so that's what I did. Whether they're zombies or young lovers, I don't care. I want people to see my stories. I love watching actors bring my stories to life."

"But that isn't life," I said. "It's pretend."

He laughed. "Of course it is," he said. "We get to make shit up for a living. How cool is that? And we get to hang out with the rich and famous."

"I don't care about the rich and famous," I said. "I don't. I don't want their approval. I don't want to know them."

"But Brooke, we are the rich and famous now," he said.

I laughed. "Maybe rich but no one in the real world could name a single screenwriter."

"That's right," he said. "Our stories become part of the communal zeitgeist. Like public art."

I looked at him. He seemed so animated. I had thought less of him because he cared about his work: I had thought his work was trivial.

"We're storytellers," he said. "I thought we were living our dream."

He was right. I was the one who was unhappy. I was the one whose son had died. I was the one who had the first affair. I was the one who had had countless affairs.

Maybe not countless.

But a bushel full at least.

I rubbed my face.

Hayword said, "The problem is that you don't love me any more. And you don't know how to let go."

My chest felt tight.

I sighed.

I looked at Hayword. He was right. I had thought he was oblivious, obtuse, kiss-ass. But he was kind, loving, and a little obtuse. He was happy with himself and his life. He had waited for me for a long time.

"I always thought that you had chosen this life over me," I said. "I blamed you. But the truth is, I walked away. I was unhappy and I didn't try to fix it. I walked away."

Oh man.

"You always came first, Brooke," he said. "I had to do what I had to do to keep the family afloat. I'm sorry if I failed."

I got up and sat next to him. I put my arm across his shoulders.

"You didn't fail, Hayword," I said. "You didn't fail."

I did.

I failed.

Now what could I do about it?

Suddenly the door flew open and my children came running in, followed by Eartha and a bit of daylight and cool air.

I could smell smoke.

The wind slammed the door shut again.

"Mom, Dad!" David said. "There's a tsunami coming!"

"What?" I said.

"I heard on the way down here about an earthquake somewhere in the Pacific," Hayword said. "They didn't mention a tsunami."

"It was on the news at the donut place," Eartha said, "and David got it on his phone."

"I have a disaster alert app," he said.

"Of course you do," I said.

"We should get up the hill to our house," Hayword said.

Eartha said, "We can't. Didn't you feel the wind? There are trees down everywhere. We could see fire, too."

"There's a huge tree down on this road," Fern said. "We couldn't even get all the way back here. We left the car and climbed over the tree."

"Shit," I said. "Armageddon is coming to a village near us."

I felt a little bit of panic.

What to do? What to do?

"David, you've had all those drills," I said. "What did you learn?"

"For smoke you should cover your mouth with wet cloth and get down low. For fire, I think you can get into a swimming pool. And for a tsunami, you need to get to high ground."

"Okay," I said. "We don't have a swimming pool, but we can get wet towels. Kids, go into the bathroom and wet towels down for us. And I think I can get us to high ground."

"When's the tsunami supposed to get here?" Hayword asked.

Eartha looked at her watch. "In about fifteen minutes."

"Let's move it," Hayword said.

Fern and David came out of the bathroom with a wet towel for each of us. We put the towels around our necks so that it would be easy to put them over our mouths.

We hurried outside. The sun was coming up, so the sky was beginning to lighten.

"Where to?" Hayword said.

"Your car."

We piled into the car, and then I told Hayword where to go. He drove us to a spot about a block and a half away. We parked on the side of the street. I pointed to the sign: Trailhead 405.

"You lead," Hayword said. "I'll be last to make sure everyone gets up."

"Can you walk up with your ankle?" I asked.

"I'm fine," he said. "Thanks for asking."

I nodded. I'd never been up this trail before. I started running as fast as I could, considering we were going up a steep incline. I glanced back to make certain the kids were right there behind me. Eartha. Then Hayword.

Trees swayed all around us. I could smell the smoke, but it wasn't thick. I put the towel near my mouth.

I couldn't run for very long. I was soon out of breath.

"Fern, you and your brother keep going up the trail, put the towel over your nose and mouth if you smell the smoke."

I didn't know if that was the right thing to do, but that's what I told them.

"But make certain you can breathe!"

Then I hurried behind them.

Eartha passed me.

The wind didn't howl, but it was noisy. The trees seemed to be swaying too much. I hoped one of them didn't fall on us. I remembered Joan telling me once that she didn't like nature because she was certain it was going to kill her one of these days. "Something is always waiting to git ya!" she said.

Something *was* always out there to git ya no matter where you were.

Hayword put his hand on my back, letting me know that he was there, spurring me on.

The trees thinned out.

The sun was turning the sky blue. The smoke seemed to be clearing.

We walked and ran.

And then we were at the top of the hill. Mountain?

We could see the village below us and the ocean beyond that.

I turned around to see the trees and mountain below and behind us.

I could see the whole world.

"Wow," Fern said. "I've never been up here. It's beautiful."

The sun coming up over the mountain was turning everything gold.

Suddenly I thought of *Beauty and the Zombie.* I began taking off my shoes. I glanced at Hayword. He smiled. He knew what I was doing.

"Dad, Mom," Fern said.

"Come on," I said. "Take off your shoes and socks, stand on the dirt, and face the sun."

My son sat on the dirt and took off his shoes and socks. Fern did the same, standing up. Eartha kicked off her shoes. She was barefooted beneath.

The five of us stood next to each other, on the cool dirt. We turned from the ocean and faced the sun. I raised my hands up to the sky.

The sun warmed my face and cooled my feet.

All was still for a moment.

I stretched as tall as I could, and I said, "Happy birthday, Alberto! I'll never forget you, darlin'! I love you. I'm so glad you were born."

"Happy birthday, son." Hayword.

"Happy birthday, brother." Fern.

"Happy birthday, Al." David.

"Happy birthday, baby boy." Eartha.

I heard footsteps on the gravel dirt and I turned around. One of the disheveled young men in business suits I had seen wandering the 'hood was standing behind us. He was taking off his shoes and socks.

"Did you hear about the tsunami, too?" he asked.

He came to stand by us, shoeless. He stared at the bay. We all turned and looked toward the ocean.

"There it is," he said.

I could see a slight rise in the water as the wave came ashore. Saw some boats lift up and bump each other.

Didn't look like the water went too far in. From up here, it seemed almost peaceful.

Ah, perspective.

David was filming it all with his camera phone. "This is great," he said. "It'll look dramatic close-up."

Another disaster diverted.

Or averted?

"Are you all right?" I asked the young man. "I've seen you walking around the neighborhood the last few days."

The young man nodded. "Sure. I'm all right. They're going to film a zombie movie in this area. At least that's what I heard. I'm getting into character for the audition. Figured zombies wouldn't be afraid of the dark, so I came out early this morning when it was still dark. Kind of spooky."

Hayword and I laughed.

"But this was the first time I've been out here," he said. "I don't know who else you've been seeing. Hey, before I got here I thought I heard someone call my name."

"What's your name?" Fern asked.

"Alberto," he said.

"Your name is Alberto?" I asked.

He nodded.

I went up to him and put my hands on his cheeks. I looked into his eyes.

Would Alberto have grown up to look something like this young man?

Where was Alberto now? Was his beautiful little spirit in some other body?

I put my arms around this young man named Alberto, and I held him against my body, held him close, like I would never get to hold my son.

He didn't try to get free. He put his arms around me and held me for as long as I held him.

When I let him go, he said, "Thanks. I have been missing my mom lately." He smiled. "I think it's safe now. I guess I'm ready to get back to the land of the living."

He slipped his shoes back on and started down the trail.

My children came up to me and put their arms around me. I began to weep. Hayword and Eartha embraced the three of us.

We all wept.

After a while, we let each other go.

I said, "I guess I'm ready to get back to the land of the living, too."

We walked down the mountain together.

TWELVE

I went into rehab again. This time to a different place, away from the city.

When I came home, Hayword and I decided to live apart, at least for the time being. They encouraged us not to make any life-changing decisions right after we got out of rehab, but Hayword and I decided it was for the best.

I repainted the bungalow, inside and out. Fern, David, and Hayword helped. Got rid of the old furniture and bought new. Let Fern and David help me choose pictures for the walls. We changed it from a love nest into a home.

I rewrote *Zombie Town* into *Beauty and the Zombie,* and everyone loved, loved it. (When can you start the rewrites?) I began script doctoring for other people besides Hayword. And I started a couple scripts of my own.

David stayed with me half the time and with Hayword the other half.

Eartha taught Hayword and me how to cook and make nonalcoholic margaritas. Hayword and I helped Violeta find another job. Not that she needed our help, but we didn't want to leave her in the lurch.

Production started on *Beauty and the Zombie*. We made sure Alberto got a part in it. Some days I took David to the set. It was a lot of fun watching people say my words.

Some months later, Joan called me to tell me she was having trouble with the plumbing in her kitchen. She had called Mark Pantano and told him she would be out of the house when he arrived. Beatriz would let him in.

He was going to be there between ten and noon on Wednesday, in case I cared.

I waited until eleven before I drove up to the house.

Mark's white truck was parked in the drive, and he was standing next to it, looking for something in the side toolboxes.

I pulled my car up behind the truck, parked it, and got out.

He turned to see who it was. I couldn't tell if he was relieved or alarmed when he saw who it was.

He set down whatever was in his hand and looked at me.

I smiled.

"Hello," I said. "My name is Brooke McMurphy. I used to live in this neighborhood. I'm a friend of Joan's. My husband lives across the street. I live in the village. I haven't had a drink in almost nine months. I write zombie movies."

He chuckled and shook my outstretched hand.

And then he quickly let go of it.

"Your turn," I said.

He rolled his eyes. "I see some things haven't changed," he said. "Still telling me what to do. Okay, my name is Mark Pantano. I don't live anywhere near here. I have a son and an ex-wife. And . . . I have a significant other."

I felt a flutter in my stomach.

Oh.

It should have occurred to me that Mark hadn't been sitting around waiting for me.

I hadn't wanted that or expected it.

I mean, Hayword and I weren't divorced. We didn't know if we would divorce.

Although we had agreed to see other people.

I looked at Mark.

"I'm pleased to meet you," I said. "And I wish you all the best. I'm so glad that you're happy."

Time for a graceful exit.

I was glad I'd gotten to see him one more time. He was still beautiful, body and soul.

I went to hug him goodbye. He embraced me, too. We held onto one another.

Then he let me go.

"Hell, I was lying," he said. "There's no one else. I've been waiting for you to get your shit together to see if we had a shot."

I slugged him in the arm. "That's mean," I said. "And for your information my shit is far from together, but I'm working on it."

We put our arms around each other again, and then we kissed.

I hadn't realized how much I had missed him.

Did this mean I loved him, really loved him?

"Joanie's been helping me look at real estate, by the way," I said. "She found this building on the coast, in a small town north of here. There's a place for a small restaurant on the first floor, already equipped and ready to go, and there's an apartment on the second floor, complete with a deck that looks out at the ocean. I've been envisioning myself on that deck, sitting by the dock of the bay. I'd need someone to open a restaurant there, in the space below the apartment—just in case you know anyone who might be interested."

"Aren't you a little ahead of the game?" he asked.

I shrugged. "I always am."

So where does this story end? With a list of what happened to the players? I always like that.
So here goes:

David doesn't mind if I spend the night away from home now, after Fern told him that it had been her suggestion that had so terrified him.

Fern finished her master's degree and then got a job as an assistant to Sally St. James. She wants to work within the system to change things. I told her that was a fool's errand. She accused me of never supporting her. So I said, "You go for it, dear."

Hayword is now executive producing. He's writing, too, and we cowrite some scripts together. He is dating. I think he had a crush on Eartha, but he never told her.

Eartha closed her business and began riding the rails. She promised us she'd get in touch when she returns to the area.

Katie Williams came out as a lesbian and left her husband. Melissa Pearce and Katie now live together.

Mark's mother Margaret seems to still like me. Giovanni, Mark's brother-in-law, now has a job as a lawyer at AFT, Sally's studio.

Sally St. James and her husband are still together. She has stopped smoking, as far as I know.

The mysterious skin disease plaguing the area has not yet gone into remission. The PR department at AFT is using it as best they can to promote *Beauty and the Zombie.*

Mark Pantano is seriously considering opening a restaurant in my new building.

And me? How does this end for me?

In the last scene of the movie of this part of my life, I am watching another sunrise.

The audience sees my back first and then the camera pans around to my front. I am holding the script of *Beauty and the Zombie: Part Two: Escape from Alcatraz*—and I look very afraid.

And then I laugh my ass off.

The End.

Kim Antieau has written many novels, short stories, poems, and essays. Her work has appeared in numerous publications, both in print and online. Her work has twice been short-listed for the James Tiptree Award and has appeared in many best-of-the-year anthologies. Critics have admired her "literary fearlessness" and her vivid language and imagination. Her first published novel, *The Jigsaw Woman,* is a modern classic of feminist literature. She is also the author of many other novels, including *Church of the Old Mermaids. Her Frozen Wild, Butch, The Fish Wife,* and *The Blue Tail. Broken Moon*, a novel for young adults, was a selection of the Junior Library Guild. Kim lives in the Pacific Northwest with her husband, writer Mario Milosevic.

Learn more about Kim and her writing at www.kimantieau.com.